THE SHADOW FALLS

Recent Titles by Michael Shea include:

BERLIN EMBASSY
BRITISH AMBASSADOR

THE SHADOW FALLS

Michael Shea

This title, complete with new material,
first published in Great Britain 1999 by
SEVERN HOUSE PUBLISHERS LTD of
9–15 High Street, Sutton, Surrey SM1 1DF.
Previously published 1975 in Great Britain and the USA
as *The Shadow Falls* under the pseudonym *Michael Sinclair*.
This title first published in the U.S.A. 2000 by
SEVERN HOUSE PUBLISHERS INC of
595 Madison Avenue, New York, N.Y. 10022.

Copyright © 1975, 1999 by Michael Shea

All rights reserved.
The moral right of the author has been asserted.

British Library Cataloguing in Publication Data

Shea, Michael, 1938-
   The shadow falls
   1. Hitler, Adolf, 1889-1945 - Death and burial - Fiction
   2. Neo-Nazism - United States - Fiction
   3. Suspense fiction
   I. Title
   823.9'14 [F]

   ISBN 0-7278-5483-6

All situations in this publication are fictitious and
any resemblance to living persons is purely coincidental.

Printed and bound in Great Britain by
MPG Books Ltd, Bodmin, Cornwall.

One way to write about diplomacy but to ensure that national and international feelings remain unruffled, is to put something of the truth into novel form. But while the settings are as true to life as possible, the characters in this book bear no relationship to persons living or dead, nor do the events to anything that has recently taken place.

INTRODUCTION

I wrote this, my fourth novel, *"A Long Time Sleeping"* now re-titled here as *"The Shadows Fall"*, over the years 1973 and 1974. At that time, I was a professional Diplomat – a member of the British Foreign Service – serving as Head of Chancery, or number two, in the British Embassy in Bucharest, Romania. I had already served as First Secretary in the Embassy in Bonn, in the Foreign Office, and on secondment to the Cabinet Office, so I had already had a fair range of activity and experience behind me. I wrote under the pen name *Michael Sinclair* because, in those days, the Foreign Office preferred their diplomat-authors to be anonymous. In writing the book, I did as I have always done, and wrote about a life and environment which was very familiar to me. While the book was written some twenty-five years ago, it is still very much up to date in terms of the way things work in diplomacy.

The central theme concerning former Nazis was not as common a one in the literature of spy fiction as it later became. I had come across quite a number of these former followers of Hitler in my career who still seemed to long for the bad old days. This was particularly true among the German expatriate community in South America.

The book translated into several languages, and while I was in Romania, I sold it to a publishing house there. These were the days of President Ceausescu and his secret police, and I later discovered that the book was censored in translation in ways that were more amusing than sinister. Ceausescu's communist regime saw fascists everywhere and any suggestion that they were still a threat had to be met with a disclaimer that the book was pure fiction!

The book was very well received at the time and I am delighted that it has now reappeared in this new edition from Severn House.

© Michael Shea August 1999

Preface

SUNDAY, AUGUST THIRTEENTH, 1967 was cool and overcast in most of south-east England. People took coats to church, but the rain stayed away and after lunch they were able to mow dry suburban lawns. In Paris, following his latest television and radio broadcast, President de Gaulle's personal popularity was at its lowest ebb. Further afield, in Cairo, President Nasser was continuing his secret talks with the Minister of External Affairs of the South Arabian Federation, light relief in the wake of his previous week's purge of around six hundred Egyptian Army officers in the bitter aftermath of the Six-Day War. In strike-paralysed Aden, Arab nationalists were pounding mortar bombs on British installations, while round the back of the world, American bombers in their turn were devastating rail links north of Hanoi, and Chinese Red Guards were continuing to hold a Soviet ship in the harbour of Talien. Across the Atlantic, Senator Fulbright was quoted in the Sunday papers as having said: "There may come a time when Americans will again be able to commend their country as an example to the world and, more in hope than confidence, I retain my faith that there will. But to do so right at this moment would take more gall than I have." On the sports pages they were reporting the end of the first U.S. professional soccer season, and the embarrassing successes the Americans had gained at the Fifth Pan-American Games, where they won a hundred and twenty gold medals, while the other thirty-five competing countries won only fifty-one among them.

On that day, at around seven on a warm and already

humid morning, a black Mercedes ambulance drove out of the main gates of a private clinic, the Wolfgang Schuster Memorial Clinic, in a rich suburb of Philadelphia. The thin layer of overnight dust was blown off the paintwork and windscreen as the vehicle gathered speed and drove west. Two men were in the front; a middle-aged driver and a much older man, both in dark suits and black ties. In the back, two other old men, black coated and erect, sat with knees uncomfortably hard against the oak and bronze chest. A large Mercedes limousine followed closely behind the ambulance. It contained five other men, three old, again all in black, all staring ahead with a strangely similar grief. No-one spoke.

It had been an important death that night; it had also been expected. The two doctors had bowed their heads by the bed at the end of the struggle at 4.48 a.m. The respiratory equipment and the glucose drip-feed stand were detached and wheeled away from the bed. The elderly night Sister with the sparse upper-lip moustache, who had, for the past seven and a half months, controlled the private wing with an iron dedication, stood in the background beside a white commode on which was a great vase of flowers. Unaccustomed tears showed in the corners of her hard eyes. Nine years of geriatric nursing of the same patient, as he grew more and more cantankerous yet more and more pitiful in his ageing, lay behind her. But now her memories predated and erased these recent symptoms; she remembered the real man.

It took an hour and twenty minutes to drive to the estate. Ten minutes were taken up at a road block where the State police were searching vehicles after a jail-break. But there was no mistaking the grief in the faces of the party and the police quickly let them through. They would not have found what they wanted beside the shrunken corpse in its coffin even if they had searched the vehicles as thoroughly as they should have done.

The high gates were open and the keeper gave a salute as they drove past. Five soberly dressed people came out of the house to greet the party; only one was a woman. A small group; they knew each other; it was almost a family affair. Six men carried the chest statefully up the seven marble steps, in through a pillared doorway, across a black and white tiled hallway hung with hunting trophies, to a room, a small darkened room, about three metres by seven, with a raised platform in the middle. A temporary chapel; but it had no true cross, no stained glass, nor font nor altar. There was only the other cross, in black against the flag. Four great church candles standing at each corner gave the only light. The windows were curtained in black velvet. It had been prepared for the lying-in-state two months previously when the end had appeared to be in sight.

The group that had accompanied the coffin from Philadelphia, their work completed, went for breakfast. It was a sober, formal affair. No-one spoke about the dead man; they all ate heartily a good American breakfast, and there was brandy at hand as required.

During that day and the two that followed, perhaps fifty people filed in and out of the little room. They stood in vigils of up to an hour before leaving. One old man stayed in a corner all day, and had to be helped away at the end of the evening. About half of the visitors came from far away, in unseasonable clothes, skins leathery with their exposure to the sun. The fatter, better dressed Europeans, ten or a dozen of them, came together, having flown the Atlantic in a rich man's private plane. One or two desultory telegrams passed between the intelligence liaison officers of a number of Western countries who noticed this joint exodus of some known, carded names, but no further reports came in and no follow-up action was taken.

On the fourth day, some thirty people were present for the interment. A two hundred yard walk along a hedge-lined path to a secluded aspen-circled clearing. A great black block of polished marble two metres high was already in place. A stone vault below it had an open door of bronze and inside, a few flowers, a flag and a plume of laurels. The vault door was heavy, the lock with three complex keys. They would represent three decisions to be taken by three different men, sometime or never, if the coffin with its contents were to be moved to where they rightfully belonged.

The coffin was placed inside; the doors were locked. The thirty stood in an orderly curve around the black marble. There was no music, no bugle, no sermon, no address, no prayer, no benediction. Two minutes silence with bowed heads then slowly, one after the other, the familiar salute.

And there was no name on the grave.

The fourth of December, 1967, was misty and cold. The blades of the two helicopters stirred the naked branches of the elder trees into a frantic dance as they roared low over them and down on to the immaculate lawn in front of the house. The three police cars sped up the drive their sirens wailing in the dawn. A rabbit crossed rapidly in front of the last police car, hesitated too long and was killed by the fourth car, a long black Chevrolet with three men in it.

The house was empty with the exception of a caretaker and his hysterical wife. The owner and any other occupant who might once have lived there had gone. They had been out of the country for some months, the caretaker explained. He had had no recent contact, indeed he had met his employer, a Mrs Rupert Bracht, on only one occasion; he had been engaged for just a short time and the house had already been empty when they moved in. His salary was paid through the bank in fortnightly instalments.

The FBI men searched the house competently. It was

tastefully and expensively furnished, but there were no personal effects whatsoever. The large library, with books in many languages, suggested a Catholic taste, but no names of any significance were written on the fly-leaves of any of them. The only thing the men removed were the stubs of the bank payment slips the caretaker had received; it did them little subsequent good since Mrs Bracht's account was a lump sum account with only the caretaker paid from it. On Mrs Bracht herself there was no further information.

Meanwhile, the other FBI men from the two helicopters were searching the grounds. At twenty-five past eight they found the mausoleum of black marble in the grove among the trees. They approached it with care as was their training. The heavy bronze metal door was unfastened and the tomb itself was empty.

Had there been more manpower, more time, more leads to go on, the investigation might have been pursued further. But in the nature of things all three were lacking, and the FBI reports were neatly filed away and forgotten.

CHAPTER ONE

West India Docks, London, E.14

SOME FOUR AND a half years later: a man is running, a slouched halting pace, but urgent with the impetus of fear. The lamps along the perimeter fence are widely spaced, and it is only when the man comes directly underneath a light that one can see that he is old; too old, too emaciated and frail to be running, too old to bear the fear a letter brought, fear etched deep into the wrinkles of the skin around his eyes.

From time to time he glances behind him into the darkness but he keeps on running. His breath forces itself in and out in thin rattles. His mouth, below the wistful, old-fashioned moustache, is dry; there is no sweat on his forehead despite the gentle warmth of the night, for the slight, desiccated body has no excess moisture left in it. It is a body that has sweated more than most in its lifetime, in the heavy green humidity that hung permanently in the air around the white house by that other river.

High blackened brick walls of the warehouse. The ship should be berthed about here somewhere. Corrugated iron roofs gleaming dully in the moonlight; moonlight also on the scum and flotsam-covered oily water as it slaps lazily against the hewn stones on the wharf. Out towards the entrance of the dock a searchlight from a river police patrol boat glides slowly across the polluted water.

The old man is tiring; his limp is more noticeable, the smartly-pressed but baggy light tweed trousers flap less frequently against the ankles of his tan laced boots. The remains of the grey hair, usually neatly plastered to the skull, blow gently in unaccustomed freedom. Where is the ship? It was not due to sail for another hour.

He looks behind again; his bad foot catches on a projecting cobble-stone. The sound of his head coming in contact with the ground is slight, like a spent eggshell crumpled against the side of a dustbin. The old man lies still. He has chosen a quiet, secluded place to die. The weeds grow thick on either side of the path and the warehouse beside it will be empty and unattended for the next few weeks until the arrival of a new cargo of phosphate from Chile brings to it a brief activity again.

1972 had a wretched summer, and it rained heavily in these next weeks; on the few dry days a constant, choking mist of dust blew across the dock from the demolition site. By the time the body was brought to the mortuary at Cottage Street E.14, for brief examination, the smartness of the tweed suit and tan laced boots had been well camouflaged and stained. The Coroner at Tower Hamlets had every excuse, when, at 10.05 on Tuesday, the first of August, 1972, he listed, almost without question, the death of an unknown down-and-out. There was nothing in the pockets; the only odd features were the silver cuff-links, the unworn cuffs and collar of the shirt, the well-made tweed suit, perhaps stolen or someone's simple charity to an old man.

The body was in need of burial, and the police, with an IRA bomb threat on their hands, had more urgent matters to attend to. The solitary reporter present at the Coroner's hearing did not bother to take a note of the proceedings.

Sir Geoffrey Benner, M.P., Germany

Twenty-five miles east-north-east of Kiel; Thursday the

third of August, 1972. The Baltic's temperamental morning winds had given place to a steady breeze, tailor-made for the huge catamaran. It foamed across the water at around eight knots, yet in the main cabin the generous Campari-sodas in their squat Danish goblets showed no danger of spilling.

The morning had been different. The catamaran *Roland* had pitched in an uncomfortable wavelength, and of the two English guests one had preferred to stay in his berth, the other had sat in the cockpit, facing into the wind, teeth clenched, determined to let fresh air kill incipient seasickness. It had been touch and go with both, but the wind eased, the seas dropped and the guests retained their dignity, though neither over-ate at the lunch of smoked salmon and cold lobster salad. Later, the bitterness of the Camparis removed the last traces of unease and they began to enjoy the sail.

The owner, who since the War had called himself Wolfgang von Neumann, or Professor Wolfgang von Neumann to be precise, and he always was precise, teased his guests in a bluff, un-German way, for their lapse from the best traditions of a nation of seamen. The Professor, a tall sparse man with an Einstein-like shock of pure white hair, made a thing about his un-German, European approach to life. He spoke English with an amusing replica of an Oxford accent; only occasionally did his vowels slip. At times in the past, occasions which he remembered with pride, he had been taken for an Englishman by other Englishmen, and even by one Englishwoman. In outlook now he was the essence of the liberal academic, tolerant of the most extreme forms of student protest, a frequent protester himself on slightly less daring political issues. A popular figure, *Der Spiegel* magazine had once dug up less amiable snippets of his past, about his work in the propaganda machine of the Third Reich, and had threatened to publish. They had not done so, not out of any fear of legal action by him, but because, when they told him of their discovery, he had, with all apparent honesty, added to their story, told more things against himself than they had believed they could have found out and then ruined the newsworthiness of the affair by publishing the lot before they could, in a student magazine of limited circulation, complete with an analytical study by himself of his past motivations. A brief sensation at the university, it was no longer national news, and Professor von Neumann's stature was enhanced rather than lowered as a result. This glib honesty won him friends and acclaim in the most critical circles.

Of the Professor's two guests, one was important and looked important even in his casual towelling shirt and rust-coloured sailing slacks. A well preserved seventy-one years, almost as tall as the Professor, with a rich man's tan and a careful man's lean figure. Clear grey eyes in an arrogantly intelligent face and a voice and demeanour that evinced familiarity with power. It was difficult to believe that this man, so obviously in command of himself, could have been weak enough to have felt sea-sick.

The other guest was different. He was a foot shorter, five years younger but his pale, lined face and scant hair suggested that he was the older. Tortoiseshell-rimmed, owl-shaped glasses and soft little hands folded neatly on his lap in front of him like a first communicant, gave him the appearance of a timid schoolteacher. That was what he was. The important guest had lived life well, more than one marriage lay behind him; the man in the glasses on the other hand was a life-long bachelor. He was equally ill-at-ease with Campari and with being on a yacht at all. His life was the occasional dry sherry and his room of books.

The German professor and his two English guests sat in the cabin talking in a cultured, old-world way. The language was English though both guests would have been happy speaking German. On deck, three of the Professor's young male students manned the tiller and and sheets and watched the set of the sails. As they were not using the engines, the engineer, who had replaced the Professor's usual mechanic, lay stretched out on the deck beside them, sound asleep. The three young men were happy at the opportunity of handling the magnificent boat; down below, the three old men were on the whole content as well.

The Professor interrupted a conversation about the fortunes of the decadent English stage and pushed a copy of the previous day's *Times* towards the important man. Wednesday the second of August's airmail edition would have carried the finding of the Tower Hamlets Coroner's Court had the death of a fourth old man been an important story.

"Look at that front page, Geoffrey," said the Professor, his white hair shaking as he made his point. "IRA, Northern Ireland in ruins, dock strikes, trade union anarchy, floating pound, inflation, stagnation. The sick man of Europe gets even sicker. A year or two ago I thought the *Englishe Krankheit* was a thing of the past."

The man called Geoffrey, Sir Geoffrey Benner, Conservative MP for Cronedale (West), shrugged distantly and said nothing. The Professor was aware of his views already and he was not one to waste his breath. The guest in the glasses, plain Mr Adrian Coles, pursed his lips and his eyes widened a little behind his lenses as if he had only now become aware of the gravity of the situation.

"By German standards I am away to the left. My students respect and listen to my views, so I must be of the left, must I not? But I could not in England tolerate to live."

"... tolerate to live in England," Benner corrected the Professor's word order and the latter frowned.

"Tolerate to live in England with such anarchy, such, such ... lack of direction," the Professor finished lamely.

"Times change, indeed they do," responded Adrian Coles after a moment, refolding his hands carefully on his lap as he spoke. The spinster-like remark was typical. Similar throw-away lines from Adrian Coles had deceived many people in the past. Generations of public schoolboys to whom he had taught Tacitus and Livy and Kennedy's Latin Grammar had in their time briefly laughed and more often than not found out their mistake more quickly than some of his life-long colleagues. He took off his spectacles, blinked, and began ferociously polishing the lenses with one end of his tie. Salt spray had left white crystals on the glass and the unfashionably thin tie, so out of place on the catamaran, had its use at last.

"Is Parliament in recess?" asked the Professor, ignoring Coles.

"Not until next week," replied Sir Geoffrey. "But I'm paired with some miner from South Wales who's got silicosis. Happy as I am to be at this delightful reunion, I have to get back tomorrow. I promised the Chief Whip. Bits of Common Market legislation to tidy up. You left the EEC out of your list of crises, Wolfgang."

"That's the Labour Party's crisis."

"I am a keen European, I always have been," Sir Geoffrey smiled, "but as you know, some of my colleagues on the right feel that we're being sold down the river or up the Rhine or Seine, or..."

"No, you've never been a narrow Nationalist, Geoffrey," the Professor smiled back.

Adrian Coles replaced his spectacles on his nose, brushed the tail of his tie flat and interrupted. "I have been paying more attention to the Common Market of late. In my view it is too diffuse, too, how shall we say, Latin."

"As a classicist, that should be an attraction to you." The Professor was still smiling. "We know your attitude to race, Adrian. You would have been a great asset to the Third Reich."

"Yes, I always believed I would," said Adrian Coles simply. He did not return the smile. Sometime in a dimly unhappy childhood little Adrian had been told severely to stop smirking, and he had seldom shown pleasure since. When he was amused, which was infrequently or when he was pleased and contented, which at times was almost a daily occurrence, the only visible sign was a little nerve that began twitching just below his left eye. For his pupils, the nickname 'Twitcher Coles' was a natural. He was twitching now.

"We should be on deck. The sun is beautiful." The Professor moved away from the table towards the hatch.

"How long before we reach Kiel?" asked Sir Geoffrey.

"With this wind..." the Professor paused, pushed his head through and shouted the same question to the student at the helm.

"Eight to ten knots, Herr Professor," the boy shouted back, glancing down at the plastic-covered British Admiralty chart in front of him. "I should think about two hours. She's sailing magnificently." The engineer still slept.

"Good. I'm coming up in a minute to take over, unless you, Geoffrey, would like to?" The Professor drew his head back into the cabin as he spoke. Sir Geoffrey shook his head. Adrian Coles was not offered the opportunity, nor would he have taken it. He was contentedly and professionally watching the helmsman through the hatch. Fair, windswept hair, most attractive, but much too long, that would not have been permitted, Coles thought. Beside him his Campari and soda remained untouched.

"We must discuss the Common Market properly some time. But it's more important that we solve some of our outstanding taxation problems before you leave," the Professor said. "But now, fresh air and sun. Come Adrian, you too on deck. I know you're not a great health addict, but it will do you good. You'd have found your mistrust of the sportsman rather out of place in the old days."

Adrian Coles showed as little irritation as he showed happiness. But there was no nervous twitch and he was not amused.

"Where the cause is right, I am prepared to tolerate others indulging in physical excess," he said precisely. After a moment's hesitation, the other two, guessing that a joke had been made, laughed. But there was no subsequent response from Adrian Coles, and to cover up the momentary hiatus, all three made their ways up on deck.

In the cockpit, the Professor took the tiller. The students tactfully withdrew to sunbathe on the fore-deck. A quick-sailing hour passed. Adrian Coles almost fell asleep in the hot sun. Once or twice his hand came up to loosen his tie, to undo the top button of his unfashionable nylon shirt. But each time some old fear of mockery stopped him—boys laughing at his flimsy physique in some vaguely remembered incident beside a swimming pool during his first year as a teacher. Once revealed twice shy.

The Professor interrupted the peace. "When did Arendt come to see you?" he asked in a low voice.

Sir Geoffrey glanced at the students and the sleeping engineer. "Some weeks ago."

"How did he find you?"

"I am well known in Britain; quite popular in some circles. And, unlike some, I have never felt the need to change my name. He came to the House of Commons."

"You recognised him?" The Professor was irritated.

"I recognised him."

"And he wanted money?"

"What else?" Sir Geoffrey stared towards the distant coastline. "He said he had a diary."

"You gave him money?"

"You always believed in the weakness of the British. Of course I did not."

There was a pause. "So?" asked the Professor, after some time. "What did you do?"

"He came to see me at the House, as I said. I saw him in the Central Lobby, hardly the most private of places. He acted out what he was: a frightened little clerk trying to do something too big. He was out of his depth."

"You were not worried?"

"Startled, yes. Worried, no. I had too many other things to think about and one of my constituents was waiting for me. I made a note of the name of his hotel and said I would contact him."

Again there was a pause, then Sir Geoffrey went on: "I did not see him again, but you could say that he received a clear message; a warning in the old style. We'll hear no more from him."

"Why are you so sure? He summoned up enough courage to call and see you after all these years."

"No, he was in Britain on private business, and tried to pull a quick trick. He came to threaten, and while the threat contained in the message I sent him was more final than I could personally deliver in law-abiding Britain, he's not to know that. He was old, he was nervous—you could see he had put on his best, perhaps his only, suit to come and see me—and when he got my message, unless I am a very poor judge of men, he'll have signed on the first boat he could and scuttled away back to his jungle."

"And the diary he talked about?"

"What would a diary prove, even if it were not just the invention of a greedy, disloyal, tired mind?" Sir Geoffrey made a gesture and then, swivelling round on his anchor locker seat, turned his back on the other two to indicate that the conversation was at an end.

Some time later, the Professor, still at the tiller, pointed with his free hand. "Recognise the coastline now, Geoffrey?"

"Never saw it. Pitch black and I was below most of the

time. But keep your voice down." Sir Geoffrey glanced round at the sunbathing students and the sleeping engineer.

"Oh come. It's a long time now. By now, most men of our age are dead, so to speak."

"Memories live. Bitterness lives."

"Most poetic, but hardly realistic today," said the Professor. He kept his eyes on the trim of the sails as he spoke. "If only Wilhelm were with us now too, what a perfect reunion..."

"Enough," Sir Geoffrey responded sharply. It was more than a request and it cast a gloom over the rest of the day.

It also left Sir Geoffrey Benner undisturbed with his memories. He had almost forgotten. He had forced himself to forget. It was over thirty years ago and what had his emotions been then? What were these memories? Had he really seen himself as some younger, more glamorous Vidkun Quisling, more acceptable, more respectable in the eyes of a defeated but still independent Britain, a Britain to be born again with the new, greater ideals? And instead, what was he now: one of the leaders of the right-wing back benches in the House of Commons. A well-known figure, but ironically, almost cruelly, not because of his political beliefs but because he had once agreed, some years previously, to take part in a popular television quiz game. He had an attractive television personality—that of the elderly statesman, the father figure, the good natured commonsensical upholder of decency, clean living and defence of the establishment. He was now a public personality: he received fan mail like any teenage pop star and had a constant stream of invitations to address meetings and conferences and open fêtes. In private, he claimed to deplore and despise this vulgar popularity, but in reality it pleased his vanity to be recognised wherever he went. The day his television career began, he had broken his spectacles and had taken with him to the studio a monocle in order to be able to read the question sheets. He had tried to abandon the monocle on the second occasion, but the producer had objected strenuously, and it was now a major part of his television personality. They had offered him a huge sum to do TV commercials but he had drawn a line at that. Sir Geoffrey Benner still had some principles to live by.

"If only Wilhelm were with us now too..." What did the Professor understand? Wilhelm ... Wilhelm Schenker. When did they first meet? What had it been? Attracted by a common sense of purpose? By the young man's striking good looks—but no, no, most definitely no, it was a most masculine, most normal attraction; it had been a common sense of purpose. At a camp together in Bavaria, a long and noble summer and then, then the War.

"...no such undertaking has been received and that, consequently, this country is at war with Germany." Mr Chamberlain on the third of September 1939; a thin, reedy, tired voice. To those now over fifty, the long months from then on are part of their personal history. They were months of waiting; the phoney war. Hitler moved across Europe and from May twenty-sixth until June fourth 1941 came Dunkirk. Shortly afterwards, there were indications out of Berlin for those who cared to look for them, that Hitler, having conquered Paris, was prepared to treat for peace with Britain. He had problems enough in the east. Britain could keep her Empire unharried by the forces of the Third Reich; in return, Germany would be allowed a free hand in Europe. To most, the answer was the two sides of the V-sign; to a few there was another course.

In Britain, the Government was packing up its archives and its treasures; lorry loads of boxes and crates left London bound for remote safety from the bombs to come.

Internment camps opened their gates to welcome alike supporters along with refugees from Nazi Germany. Old men, essential home workers and boys put on the uniform of the Home Guard and practised riot drill. The tiny secret army of 'Auxiliary Units' came into being; two thousand five hundred men and women of Britain's incipient underground resistance.

Across the Channel, alongside the major plans for conquering the British Isles, Germany drew up its plans for the occupation to be. Proclamations in English were prepared; regulations were drafted to ensure that the British civil authorities continued under the German Military Government. All males between the ages of seventeen and forty-five were to be deported; assemblies were to be forbidden; there was to be a planned reduction in the food supply leading to debilitation and a consequent weakening of any potential resistance. Disobedience would be punishable by death.

The Germans had two lists prepared; the Black List of those who were potentially dangerous and who would therefore be eliminated or deported immediately following the invasion, and the White List of those who might be counted on to help.

Young Geoffrey Benner looked at his watch. The phosphorescence had almost worn off, but he could just make out the angle of the hands—five to nine—it could not be quarter to eleven yet. The gentle motion, almost imperceptible, of a ship at anchor. The smell of tar and wet sacking. It was cold, bitterly cold, but the wind was low. His duffel coat had gone and he had been given a long coat of forest green. "You can hardly wear that duffel coat," they had said. The coat was much thinner, too large for him, but the cuffs projected over his hands and helped to keep them warm.

He had not expected it to be like this, so scruffy, so

uncomfortable. Clandestine, secret, yes, but surely it could have been arranged differently? The first leg of the journey, the flight to Stockholm had been easy, the cover was perfect, they had arranged it all. Then the wait, the long wait in the bare room in a house by the Central Station. A midnight rendezvous, a short car journey, on to this ship and a cheerful cabin. An hour out they had bundled him below. Why, he had asked? They know; they're expecting me. Ask no questions, had been the reply. Too many people know already. But don't worry. It is all in order.

Black in the hold, a shimmer of a torch, a man whose face he could not make out, shaking his hand fiercely in the darkness. Stumbling up steel ladders along echoing companionways, out into the open. It was still black. Black, black, blackout, the same as in the London he had left two weeks earlier—was it only two weeks earlier? A man appeared with an Alsatian dog straining at a short chain, stared briefly at the group, and vanished. He wore a long green leather coat, the peaked cap with the bent cross, so familiar from the newsreel films and from that Bavarian summer.

He felt something cold on his face, put his hand up and felt the snowflakes. A dimmed torch cut a swathe through the night and he saw a car, long, low, soft-topped, powerful. A uniformed driver opened the rear door and he got in. Another man, he guessed it was the man who had shaken his hand in the hold, got in the other side. The doors crunched shut, an expensive well-built sound. The car was already warm. The engine must have been running until recently.

They pulled away. He could see little from behind with the blue masked headlights, except that it was still snowing. He glanced sideways, saw nothing, then realised that there were curtains over the windows. The car stopped briefly, a man in a peaked cap stood outside with an

Alsatian, perhaps the same man and dog. A gate unlocked, opened, and on they went into the night.

He attempted to speak but was motioned to silence, so he dozed off. Three hours and a stop. At a guess an army camp. A new driver; petrol in the tank. His silent companion in the back seat disappeared, then returned with a thermos of hot, excellent coffee and some sandwiches: Leberwurst. The taste brought its memories. Memories of Munich, memories of Bierkellers and the Corps. The duels, the dances, the beautiful women. He had despised the drinking, had a non-participating interest in the fencing and admired the women. He had hunted, studied, lived life to its fullest. In these days he had been popular, so popular for an Englishman. The money helped, so did his sympathy and charm. The Party had changed all that; less pleasure, but more purpose.

Leberwurst sandwiches. Coffee, so good, he hadn't tasted such good coffee since before the war, all these years ago —was it really only two, since Chamberlain's despairing voice "...no undertaking has been received and that consequently, this country ... consequently, this country ... consequently, this country is at war with Germany."

The new driver drove faster. Were they late? What time was it? Quarter past one the thin phosphorescence suggested. It could not be five past three. The new driver knew the road better; the ride certainly was smoother.

"Sleep now. Another seven or eight hours," the man beside him advised.

"Where are we going?" he asked.

"You can't expect me to say," came the enigmatic reply.

He slept. He slept well, only waking when they stopped, twice or was it three times, to refuel and to change drivers. They drove faster every time, so it seemed. About six they had a puncture. A grey light was in the sky and it was raining. They had left the snow behind up north. He stayed where he was. The driver and the other front-seat passenger struggled to change the wheel. Half awake, he could hear them cursing the car and each other. There was a clang on the road as a pistol dropped; he heard one of them say that it hadn't been damaged.

He had no dreams. He was content within himself, stimulated by his mission, the excitement, the belief in the rightness of it all, the promise of it all, the hope, the hope.

Into the dawn. His partner was sleeping; carefully he pulled back the curtain and looked out. They were passing through a waking village. A soldier on a bicycle leaving his billet and a girl with fair untidy hair waving from an upstairs window; a postman with a bag; an old woman in black, bent almost double; a pretty child carrying too large a basket of bread. The car stopped at a road junction. The child, a little girl, stopped too, staring at the big, dark car with the sinister curtains over the rear windows, like a hearse. As the car pulled away, a loaf of bread rolled out of her basket on to the wet roadway. The girl bent to pick it up, endangering the rest of her load. Then she passed from view.

The man beside him was stirring, so he let the curtain fall back into place. The man sat up with a start, looked at his watch, pulled his curtain back to see how far they had gone. "Only twenty minutes or so," he said. "We are in good time. With luck we shall have time to shave and wash. You have a clean shirt? We can have coffee, it will make us more alert. He will be up already, long ago. He works, functions best, in the morning and demands it of others. You will see."

A shiver of anticipation: he was aware of himself sitting more upright in the seat, and he blinked rapidly to clear the sleep from his eyes. He was glad about the coffee.

Through another small village then a left fork along a new, well-made road, the car passed a group of workmen in brown denim overalls building a high stone wall. With a shock he noticed the guards, guns slung over their backs, watching the labour gang. The car slowed down to take a bend and he focussed through the front windscreen on one of the workmen, a young man with an old, pale face and large, staring eyes. He was struggling to carry a large block of granite on his shoulder. He was not going to make the distance.

Two blockhouses, squat, characterless, but white and neat on each side of a red-and-white-painted swing barrier. Guards, mainly in the black uniform of the SS, rifles, high walls, searchlights mounted in watch towers. Passes produced and scrutinised, telephone calls made to higher authority, then the car and its occupants are allowed through. A drive of no more than two hundred metres, well-tended winter gardens, a second barrier, more guards, a soldier with a machinegun sitting in the little concrete nest at the top of a guard house: more checks and again a short drive. Barrack huts to the left and right, everything neat and tidy. Orderlies and servants in denim overalls, a large stone building with great bronze doors. The car pulls up outside and everyone gets out. It is a relief to be in the fresh air, to be able to stretch one's legs again. Into the building: the promised coffee is there, and the joy of a shower, a hurried shave and the opportunity to change clothes.

Through a hall hung the flags and pictures, modern, heroic pictures, along corridors with uniformed guards at ten yard intervals: there have been several assassination attempts is the whispered explanation. Into an antechamber: secretaries and aides, male and female, behind rosewood desks; telephones ringing, maps and charts along one great wall with people placing and pulling out brightly-coloured pins and flags. A young man detaches himself from a group at the far side of the room. He salutes, smiles and they shake hands. Friendship, and it is all worth while for that.

The meeting is brief. Five nervous minutes' wait on leather bench. A buzzer goes and a light goes on above a large double door at one end of the antechamber. For a second time he shakes hands quickly with Wilhelm Schenker, the doors are opened and he is ushered in to the Führer's study.

A housefly, trapped in the cabin ever since the catamaran had left harbour, escaped from its prison at last and was swept away by the wind to the brief freedom of the Baltic and its lonely death. Through half-closed eyes the engineer, still stretched out on the deck, watched it go.

Professor von Neumann looked across with distaste at the recumbent body of the engineer. The man was idle; he would not sign him on again. But the reverse was true: the engineer was working, working overtime. As a minor agent of the Federal Government investigating tax frauds he was straining his ears to catch the conversation. He was nervous, more used to a desk job, and sweat lay in little rivulets in the folds of his palms as he lay there hoping that no-one would decide to adjust the chronometer behind which the tiny bugging device was concealed.

At the end of the day the agent had gained a little more information for his department, but neither that tiny device nor his ears could pick up old men's memories.

CHAPTER TWO

Major Wilfred Turton, J.P., R.A. (Retd.), Kent

THE SUN SHONE mistily down on a Kent rose garden on Sunday, the eighth of April, 1973. Major Wilfred Turton was working behind his converted dream cottage, tidying the already meticulous beds. He was a man with an equally meticulous mind, but one that had become increasingly humdrum of late, a mind that thought as he talked, in comfortable, chatty clichés. The roses were budding well; the Major, armed with a battery of sprays and fertilizers lined up neatly in a wooden apple box, had great hopes for the Autumn Flower Show. Last year's rosettes were pinned proudly above the door of his do-it-yourself greenhouse, and he had plenty of space for new winners for this year's crop. That reminded him; he must get his wife to ask Lady Smythe round for a drink one evening soon. It was never too early to keep the Chairwoman of the Judges sweet, even though she was a bit of a gossip and namedropper.

Upstairs in the chintzy main bedroom, Mrs Ethel Turton, called Etty because the Major had always found her christian name not quite top-table enough, was spread across the bed in luxurious leisure with the Sundays. The *Observer*, with the exception of the Magazine section which had already been glanced at, lay unopened on the side table and would stay that way until it hit the dustbin. The *Telegraph* was there ready and waiting; the *Sunday Express* had already been digested or its gossip columns had, and Mrs Wilfred Turton was now engrossed in the delights of the *News of the World*. It had been one of their hardest battles. After the Major's retirement ten years earlier they had moved to Little Stapeling and had argued at length over whether they could risk Mrs Askham, the newsagent's, cold looks if they ordered that particular paper. They had taken the plunge, and once when Mrs Forsythe next door had come in and spotted it on the lounge sofa, the Major had had to force a laugh and a remark about having to see how the other half lived. Mrs Forsythe had smirked and left quickly, and a tense few weeks of disapproval had followed until Mrs Forsythe herself had been *tired* one night after a bridge evening, had hit a lamp post from which and from the law, Major Turton, gallant to the last, had rescued both her and the car. They were now the best of friends: 'neighbours in sin', the Major boisterously remarked to his wife some days later.

It was warm. The Major, looking every inch his part with his neatly bristled moustache, his cropped hair round a shiny bald patch, his carefully tied Paisley pattern neckerchief inside the checked shirt, had rejected his heavy serge trousers and the old jacket he had worn throughout the months of winter gardening, and had put on, for only the second time, the tweed suit with the history. It was rather too good for a gardening suit, but the Major still had a lurking suspicion that someone might recognise it. He played it safe, but he would risk wearing it later when he strolled with his wife down the lane to the Deep Ford Arms for a Sunday lunchtime drink.

The suit fitted him well. The Major's mind may have become a little trivial, but he had kept his figure. Etty had helped now and again by cutting down on the potatoes and rationing the intake of home-made beer. The suit was a slim fit, yet there had been no need to let out the waist.

The suit had a history. It also had a good Savile Row label inside the wallet pocket, and that was why Mrs Wilfred Turton had done the unthinkable one day when driving back from a morning's shopping in London last winter. She had stopped when she saw a church fête in progress somewhere in one of those run-down districts of outer London. It was somewhere off the South Circular Road. She went in. The church hall was stuffy and crowded. The wares for sale in support of the church's fabric were in the main scruffy in the extreme. She was about to leave when the vicar came up and spoke to her. Would she not buy something, he asked, then, noticing that she was not a local, added—or give a donation? She began to open her bag. But the Major's pension and their joint dividends were far from large and she had the canniness of her Scottish farmer father. She spotted the suit. The police had given it to the church. A member of the congregation who had a dry cleaning establishment had cleaned it free of charge; no-one there knew that for two or three weeks it had been a winding sheet. It was well made and of good quality and the size looked about right for Wilfred. Some of the stitching needed redoing, but a woman handy with a needle...

"Just the thing for the gardener," said Mrs Wilfred Turton in a voice that made the vicar look at her very hard indeed. There was a hand-written label with the price: two pounds; expensive for a Church sale which was why the locals hadn't snapped it up. Nor was that particular fox-hunting weave quite the thing in East 14. Mrs Wilfred Turton seized the suit, thrust two pounds and a new fifty penny piece for good measure into the hands of the grateful vicar, and beat a flustered retreat. She felt rather silly and upset when she got back into the safety of her old Morris Estate, but she made a virtuous charity out of her impetuously inspired necessity when she poured out her story to the Major later in the day. He had been irritated at her spending money uselessly, but later had begun joking about himself, the gardener, trying it on. It fitted well, he liked it and was not too displeased in the end.

The Major took a little bone meal and forked it in round the roots of his Princess Elizabeths and Crimson Splendours, and then reached behind him to the apple box to get his secateurs. One or two branches of dead wood had escaped his careful autumn and spring prunings, and were only now revealed by their dark colour and the absence of life and leaves on them. As he leant behind him, his sleeve caught on the prickly spines of one of his treasures. He pulled his arm away and the thread of the jacket, rotted by its exposure to the elements, tore neatly along the seam of the lower right arm. He cursed under his breath with a few well-chosen army words of anger—releasing simplicity. Disengaging the cloth from the thorns, he examined the damage. Not too bad. The cloth was intact. His wife would have no difficulty in repairing it. But what about his rose bush? It was unharmed. He stood up. Enough was enough. He would go indoors, make his wife and himself a cup of Nescafé, take it up to her and then read a paper or two before the lunchtime drink. He wondered if Tommy Skeffington would be at the pub. He wanted to ask him about his experiences with budding roses. He himself had never had much success, but Tommy claimed he hardly had a failure.

The Major left the box of tools and fertilizers in the greenhouse and went indoors. In the kitchen he took off his jacket and again examined the sleeve. He would break it to his wife after her coffee. She had been a bit upset about his reaction to the suit and might feel he had deliberately been a bit rough with it. He would play the old girl gently.

It was good material, well put together; the backing of the sleeve, the lining, was good quality too, though it would never normally see the light of day. None of your hessian, jute, sack-cloth. It was like silk.

The Major paused. He pulled at the inside. It was silk. One bit seemed to be loose. He felt it between his fingers.

Then he realised; he would know it anywhere. He had not worn that little blue and white parachute badge on his arm for nothing. He knew parachute silk when he saw it. But that was a bit old-fashioned nowadays. Artificial fibres had surely won the day. The Major pulled a bit harder. A whole piece of the silk from the inside of the sleeve came out. Shoddy workmanship after all. But no. The lining was still there. This was an extra bit of cloth, carefully sewn together into a little book, rather like those cloth books they make for very young children, only much thinner. Beautifully stitched round the edges; one page was a ... was a map. Like those escape maps they used to give air crew and SOE types, printed on to silk which folded away into nothing.

The other three pages were different, closely covered in very faint writing. It must have been difficult to write on silk. Black writing, spidery writing, strange letters some of them; no, it was Gothic script. He had been in the Control Commission in Germany from '47 to '49. He knew a bit of German. It was a diary of sorts. 1945, April; late April and May 1945. The man who had written it had flown somewhere. Where had he been at that time, Major Turton asked himself? Somewhere in Italy? Yes, he would still have been in Italy then, rounding up the last of Musso's boys. It was almost all over by then, bar the last mopping-up operations. Interesting. Why the silk diary in the sleeve? Tailors must have been hard up for material. But how silly of him; the backing was still there, and the lining was intact. The Major looked at the sleeve with a sudden spark of greater interest. Silk squares into a diary, sewn together so neatly; it must have been hidden there. Interesting. Why should anyone do that?

Major Turton took the silk sheets gently in his fingers and laid them out on a piece of blotting paper on his desk. He had read that the Imperial War Museum was collecting personal war diaries. He liked reading war diaries.

Couldn't be many written on parachute silk; it might have curiosity value at least.

It did not quite happen that way. The Major put the diary away in a fold of blotting paper inside his *Times Atlas of the World*. Two weeks later he took it out to show to Tom Pickforth, his wife's difficult but bright young cousin who was a lecturer at Sussex University. Tom was markedly interested, so interested that he forgot the Major's flagons of home-made beer he had called for. He took the diary away to study it. He agreed with the Major: it was a strange document. Could he bring it back later, in a few weeks' time? He was going abroad to a conference, to the Middle East, and he might not have time to decipher it before he left.

CHAPTER THREE

Foreign and Commonwealth Office, London, S.W.1

THE LEFT-HAND TELEPHONE rang once. It was Gilbert Winter's wife asking when he would be home. Pringle had never found much in common with Mrs Winter, but on this occasion, he sympathised. When Winter had replaced the receiver, Pringle stood up noisily. By now most people were in front of their television sets and de-frozen suppers, and, while as Desk Officer for United States affairs he used to get some vicarious pleasure out of leaving late after a hard day, recently it had been happening too often. But Winter had insisted that they get the telegram away before they left, and, as it was a complex piece of drafting which had been rendered all but incomprehensible by the Legal Advisers in the course of the afternoon, it was now twenty past seven.

He eased himself out of the room faster than decency allowed, knowing that just before the door clicked behind him, Winter had looked up with recognisable surprise from blotting his last black italic amendment. He liked to talk things over. Decorum and a studied lack of haste were old-fashioned characteristics which he said he valued and certainly practised. Even if one was late for some function in diplomatic life, it was better not to run; one arrived too breathless to say and advise in the way one might if the arrival had been slower. Too much energy was unseemly in Winter's eyes, and Pringle's confidential report was in his slim pending tray at that moment. But the invitation card read six-thirty to eight, and enough was enough. Winter would now pick himself up, stroll along the corridor to the Private Office and get the

Minister's unquestioning initial of authorisation at the bottom of the draft. Then equally slowly he would make his way home to Blackheath.

Pringle rushed up the stairs a little too fast for his incipient spare-tyre, along the cream corridor with its festoons of pipes and message-tubes that had reminded someone older than he was of the 'tween-decks of a battle-ship, to his drab second-floor office. He cleared his desk and locked his papers away in thirty seconds flat. As he scrambled the combination dial of the steel cupboard, he noticed that he had left a confidential paper lying out in one of his trays. Rather than reopen the cupboard—juggling with the temperamental combination could waste precious minutes—he sealed it up in an envelope which he addressed to himself and left it with a messenger to collect again in the morning.

The Victorian cage lift dropped him uncertainly to the ground floor and he went towards the main door. The doorkeeper called goodnight, addressing him as always by a name that was not his. Pringle thought of telling him, but he had been calling him Mr Wilson for so long that it would have unsettled the friendliness of the relationship to correct him now. Who was Wilson, and was he going through identical doubts answering to Pringle's name?

Pringle was always very careful in his dealings with junior staff. He believed that man-management was one of the most important elements in his conscious pursuit of success. But in practice, whatever his success with those below him, he was less careful and adept with his equals and superiors. He showed a mixture of arrogance and self-importance that would have made him a number of enemies in a fairly arrogant profession, were it not balanced out by a considerable ability and the odd flash of humour. Conceit made him speak out of turn, a habit that led to his good advice being ignored. Occasionally he gained a glimpse of these deficiencies in himself but so far in his thirty-five years he had done little to rectify them and it was touch and go whether he would become pompous before the cut-off age of fifty.

In the courtyard, a few cars were still parked; on the upper floors of the Office only five lights burned, among them the one from Gilbert Winter's office and the adjacent one of his long-suffering PA. On the ground floor there were more lights; on the right, the fluorescent windows glared where the Communications Centre was working up to its busiest time in the day. The Office had cleared its trays and gone home. But telegrams such as the one Winter had just completed, had to be despatched to the many British Embassies and Missions that, to the surprise of every man in the street, were ever-increasingly spattered about the globe.

Pringle made his way across the cobbles towards the King Charles Street gate. The IRA bombs of the past weeks had led to the closing of the Downing Street entrance. Those of his colleagues who lived north were irritated by this, those setting out for Waterloo or Victoria scarcely noticed. Rush hour was well past as was the time of frequent Number 3 buses. He waited fifteen minutes in the wet October night, then hailed a taxi that had just dropped a fare at the Treasury. As he sank into the seat and ordered his destination, he saw through the blue rear window an empty Number 3 rushing up and past. It was one of those days, and still two weeks away from the pay cheque.

The cocktail party in Stockwell, if such one could call it, had passed its peak. The more energetic had already booked up their parties for the delights of eating out in South London; the wine cup had run out and he was forced to drink Sainsbury's Red out of a dirty glass. A group of three, two girls and a bearded man who was well enough oiled to greet a late-coming stranger whom he did not know, blocked the doorway. The man introduced himself and started up the 'What do you do?' questions before Pringle had the glass to his lips. He saw he was out of phase with the party, his host was away stocking up his supplies from the off-licence across the road, and he thought for a moment that he might have been better nurturing his confidential report in Gilbert's office. The man with the beard was insistent. Pringle told him.

"Foreign Office, eh. Slumming it a bit south of the river, aren't you?" the man said affably. Pringle smiled politely.

"Eton and Kings, James Bond and the British Raj, that's the stuff," the man went on, exuding bad breath and bonhomie in equal doses. Pringle kept smiling. It was standard stuff.

"I knew a man once, toffy-nosed sod; he went to one of these country house selection parties you have. None of your peas with a knife for him."

"What happened?" one of the girls asked.

"Failed. He's a bloody stockbroker now. Quids in. It's a very upper place the FO isn't it?" the man addressed Pringle. His glass, held at an angle, was spilling red wine on the carpet.

"I don't know. We have to communicate with all sorts these days," Pringle said politely.

For a moment Pringle thought the man was going to hit him. Then he took it as a joke and bellowed his appreciation.

"Very good. Yes, very good. I bet you lot take courses on how to speak to wogs, eh? 'How now my good little black man. Which tree did you crawl off?'" The man roared again. Pringle kept smiling, and eventually the man pushed off, unwilling to take offence at his lack of response. He pulled one of the girls with him. Pringle was left with the other.

There was a pause and he looked round the room. "Seen John?" he asked, naming the host.

"John?—oh the man who's giving this thing you mean.

Sorry, no. Not quite sure which one he is. I was brought," she explained. Pringle smiled.

"Is that a fixture?" she asked suddenly. Pringle half turned to look behind him to see what object she was talking about.

"What...?"

"Your smile. Does it come with the job?" she spoke without obvious malice.

"Oh, I..." He took refuge behind his glass of Sainsbury's. "Well I suppose..." The girl had hit on a vague unease of his. The smile that had been attractive and boyish in his twenties was becoming a shade artificial through over-use, like an air stewardess's. Pringle had a pleasant appearance, a broad, friendly face and a middle-height figure that still looked athletic when hidden behind well-chosen Aquascutum suits. He modelled himself on a number of senior diplomats with whom he had served, picking up a habit here and a gesture there, but the amalgam was not always successful and could suggest insincerity.

"That man who's just left didn't know whether you were being pleasant or rude."

"I know. But what I said just now was meant to be funny, not offensive. We were told when we joined the Service to beware the dangers of wit and the pitfalls of humour—especially with foreigners."

"Including slightly tight Welshmen?"

"Ah, that explains a great deal. He was Welsh, was he? Welshmen are..."

"Oh for goodness sake stop grinning like that. It's so artificial."

"What did you say your name was?"

"I didn't. You mean I can't start complaining about you till we've been introduced?"

Pringle looked down at her for the first time. She was small and dark, long hair with a highly generous figure for her size. A well formed face, big eyes and no make-up. It was she who was smiling now, by no means an insincere smile, rather more mocking. She had got him on the defensive and would keep him that way if she could. He knew that much about her already. He classified women in a number of ways, sexual and intellectual. She looked at first glance as though she might score quite highly on both counts. Alert and interested in what was going on around her, she avoided the fashionable facial habit of appearing disinterested or unenthusiastic about anything. And to him, intelligence was a great aphrodisiac.

"Let's go somewhere for dinner. I've had this party," he said, hoping his unusually reckless bravado wouldn't show too much. At introspective moments, he wrongly thought of himself as a 'speak when you're spoken to' type.

"I'm attached."

"It's not too obvious."

"Over there in the corner. Tall, fair hair."

"Husband?"

"Goodness, no."

"He seems fairly attached to the girl he's with."

There was silence for a moment. The fair-haired man proved the point by wrapping himself round the girl as they watched. Pringle looked down at his companion.

"All right," she said. "Can you find my coat?"

"Name?"

"Helen."

"Oh *no*."

"Why?"

"My wife's name."

"My turn to say 'Oh no'. You're not really married?"

"Divorced."

"At least you won't murmur the wrong name in my ear as the night wears on."

He flushed. He had caught on to someone who was fairly

direct, or was pretending to be. "Ah ... yes," he said wisely.

"Thank God, you've stopped at last."

"What?"

"Grinning."

That was enough. He'd have to attack to defend, if the evening and his ego were to stand the pace. He took her arm firmly and led her out of the room. As they left he had a glimpse of her former escort as he looked across, but he did not unwrap himself from his new find. That was all right by Pringle as well.

At the door, the host, John, appeared carrying a clutch of bottles. "Hi," he said, "glad you could come." He pushed past them sweating.

"You didn't seem to know him too well either," Helen said.

"Friend of a friend." They had never had much in common and he had wondered equally at the invitation and at his decision to come.

"Where are we going to eat?"

"A small Italian Restaurant in the South Lambeth Road. Good, straightforward and no nonsense." Pringle said the first thing that came into his head. But they acted on it and ten minutes later were settled at a corner table.

"You start," she began. "Tell me, do Foreign Office men normally go about picking up strange birds at parties?"

"Constantly. Established practice." He'd try the dry approach. Slightly superior. He rapidly reconsidered his tactics when she began stiffening up. She was not the type to be upstaged or impressed in that way, and it would need a more casual approach. He wondered if he had forgotten how. Then recalling what she had just said, he noted a slight shift of vowel sounds that were not quite regional.

"You speak English perfectly," he said glibly. A touch of the cosmopolitan would do no harm.

"You think I'm not English?"

Her grammar was perfect, her pronunciation almost so. "German, probably Bavarian." He hazarded more than a guess.

"Go on, Professor Higgins."

"You'll have to talk some more. I need verbal research material to go on."

She began talking, but not about herself. It was mainly about living in London. But Pringle was too busy watching her to take it all in, and all he did was to provide some standard unthinking responses from time to time to keep her going. He forgot about analysing her speech. He would save his energy. She would tell him sooner or later.

She was not outstandingly pretty but had a lively, at times exciting face, which sparkled as she spoke, and her gestures added strength to Pringle's belief that she was anything but British. Probably about twenty-eight, well educated or at any rate well-informed, she talked on without making a single remark that jarred. After the introduction, her commentary of the London scene became equally alive and amusing. He had made a real find, Pringle told himself. Then there was her figure. It strained attractively at the simple open-necked tunic dress she was wearing, and it quickened him. She caught him staring at her and instinctively glanced down to see if she had a button adrift. She looked back up and smiled a small provocative smile that made him think what it was meant to make him think. He started listening after that; she realised, and switched again to the attack.

"What d'you think diplomats are all about?" she began sweetly.

"There's an ill-informed discussion of that every week in the press. You know the sort of thing. Letters to the Editor: 'Sir, In this age of jet travel and rapid telecommunication why should we taxpayers continue to bear the burdens...' and so on." Pringle put on his best *Daily Telegraph* voice.

She laughed.

"The public image; a mixture between George Brown and Carlton-Browne. The fact is, no-one in the street knows anything about us. You can tell from the cigarette brand names—*Ambassador, Consul, Embassy*. It's as remote and as glamorous as *Pall Mall, Sotheby's* and *Winston*, but in fact closer to *Woodbine* or *Capstan*." He felt pleased at keeping up the simile. She smiled politely.

The food with the background noise, the crowded tables and the canned music came and went surprisingly quickly and they found themselves at coffee and the bill.

"Home?" he said hopefully.

"Where's home?"

"Just round the corner. Lambeth. Easy walk to the Office. Only exercise I get."

"You sound like an old man."

"Thirty-five," he said, "and a life in ruins." He grinned.

"That smile again! It would be quite nice if you didn't force it so much. Does your wife..."

"Oh no. My former understood me too well, or thought she did. That's why we're divorced. Too alike in many ways."

"Now you sound like a woman's magazine."

Pringle changed the subject back to diplomacy. It was safer. "No-one outside knows anything about what we do. They either have an image of cocktails or spies. There's a hell of a lot else. We'd be better calling ourselves Civil Servants."

"But the popular idea of that sort of creature is a tax man or the person behind the grille in the Post Office. You at least have spies and cocktail parties to make you different. And, how many British diplomats come from Tower Hamlets?"

"Tower Hamlets is too new. But I did know one from Merseyside." The joke fell flat.

"I must go. I can't bear you grinning any more." She was teasing but serious about leaving.

"Let me take you home. I remember what you said about breathing names in your ear later." As he spoke he knew that it wasn't going to be like that. He'd take her home wherever that was, and she would leave him at the door. He was wrong.

At the word home, she looked quickly down at her watch as if she had forgotten something. Then she excused herself briefly; Pringle presumed, equally wrongly, where she was going. She spoke to a waiter who pointed, and then he saw her go through a door marked Telephone. He sat waiting, and finished the remainder of the wine rather irritably.

She returned after two or three minutes and sat down again at the table without explanation, and after a short time in which they sat more or less in silence, he paid the bill and they left together. He turned to the right, making for his Ford which was parked round a corner in a side street.

"Sorry," she said. "I have a commitment which I totally forgot. I'd better wait here."

Pringle's face fell. "Were you phoning for a taxi? I would have liked to have..."

"Something like that. I know you would. I really am sorry," she said. She looked as if she meant it, but did not explain further.

Just at that moment a large black Mercedes drew up outside the door of the restaurant and a man jumped out and came towards them. He had a chauffeur's cap on, otherwise Pringle might have jumped to conclusions. Helen had obviously expected to wait longer but was not surprised. The man said something and she replied. Pringle was at least right about her origins. It was German they spoke; he had spent hard years learning it. But he didn't catch what they said, except that she made some remark about his having been very quick.

She turned towards Pringle, smiled sweetly, and said "I'm afraid I must leave you. I have to meet a plane. Sorry. I was quite looking forward to hearing your wife's name." She stretched out her hand and he shook it politely, geared as a reflex to this by ten years in the Service. Then she moved swiftly towards the car. The chauffeur had already opened the rear door. Pringle was left gaping like an idiot. She half turned, smiled, waved and got in.

"When shall we..." he began, like the words of a pop song, but the car was already pulling away.

He stood outside the restaurant like the Prince without even Cinderella's slipper for a clue as to whom she was. Then he saw the discreet CD plate on the back of the car as it disappeared up the South Lambeth Road and knew he'd been had. Twittering on like an idiot, he'd been talking to someone who must know the diplomatic scene as well as he did. It was eleven-thirty, the pubs were shut, and, much as he had drunk of the house wine, he knew that the half inch of whisky in the bottle back at the flat was hardly sufficient to numb his frustrations.

CHAPTER FOUR

Foreign and Commonwealth Office, London, S.W.1

HE SLEPT BADLY and woke with a headache, but was in the Office by nine-thirty. A Ministry of Defence man whom he knew slightly sat beside him on the upper deck of the 159 bus, explaining his lateness as being due to some excursion with his central heating system. Pringle was early, since by long established and well defended tradition, the Foreign Office starts late and finishes late. Pringle could remember being told when he first joined that it dated from the period when the post coaches used to arrive from Dover with the diplomatic bags from St Petersburg and Berlin.

The Washington Embassy had worked their day through Pringle's night and their querulous objections were in the first distribution of telegrams. They had managed to disagree with nearly every point of substance on the grounds that to pursue the present line would both fail to appease the Americans and at the same time would seriously offend the Europeans; the Embassy in Moscow had responded with a quibble of words about likely Warsaw Pact reactions. It was hard enough trying to negotiate any damn business between countries, Pringle thought, without having our own Embassies making trouble by overestimating reactions. As if they hadn't already had enough fuss negotiating a national position with the other departments in Whitehall who felt they had to have some say in the formulation of foreign policy. It was always the hardest part where everyone thought they knew the home ground.

Gilbert Winter was on the phone by nine-forty asking

for his views. Had he done a draft reply? Had Winter not been so senior, and had Pringle's confidential report not been in his tray, he would have told him where to go. Instead, he stifled his annoyance and said he was trying to get hold of a typist to dictate to. One of the department's secretaries was at the dentist, the other was making tea, he explained. Winter, strangely, did not want to know, told him to have the draft telegram ready and come down for a meeting at ten-thirty in his room, and then put the phone down unnecessarily abruptly. Perhaps he'd had another row with his wife, but he should know that it would take most of the day to get a new draft cleared round all the departments.

A messenger came in with the envelope Pringle had left with him the night before, and also a letter of sorts from his ex-wife. It was typical of her; no heading nor signature, with her writing supposedly sufficient to indicate from whom it had come. It enclosed a bill which she claimed should be his to pay. If he had been irritated, now he was angry. The stupid bitch. She never let up. He shoved it in an envelope and sent it on to his lawyer. He could deal with it. He charged enough.

As the messenger laid the letters down on the desk he knocked over a little tray of pins, paperclips and little bits of coloured string known as Treasury tags, on to the floor. Reading the letter, Pringle ignored his grunt of apology as he noisily scrabbled about retrieving these necessary links in the process of British government. He left them in a muddle on the tray, adding a further irritation, for Pringle liked to think of himself as methodical. Three grey plastic correspondence trays—*in*, *out* and *pending*; he kept them all as empty as possible. When they were full he weeded out the rubble, the thick bundles of background reading as quickly as possible, and then got down to the problem files. Some people would start with the problems. For him it was close to psychologically essential to have a clear desk in order to think clearly.

Papers and files in the Office found their way between departments in envelopes if they were less delicate or, if sensitive, in Victorian despatch boxes about eighteen inches by a foot square, the black and less glamorous cousins of the red one waved by Chancellors on Budget Day. Those who had to use them had a key. Cumbrous but secure, there was always something satisfying to Pringle about opening one, removing the contents, untying the ribbon bundling the relevant files together, reading his way through the back correspondence and minutes, adding his own comments to a draft or submission, initialling and dating what he had written, and then thrusting the lot neatly into the box again. Reach for a label, address it to its next destination, place the label over the two brass teeth that would hold it in place when the lid was closed, shut the box, lock it and ring for a messenger to send it off, tidy and secure. No piles of papers in the out-tray to distract him.

That morning, he used the first five minutes to clear the rubble, the circulars, the despatches from posts that neither interested nor concerned him, keeping aside only one on the Middle East dispute and adding it to his pending tray to read at leisure. Then he settled down to the draft. He wrote it longhand on the margined blue paper. He knew he'd get nowhere trying to get a secretary, and in any case, even if the girl who was not at the dentist had finished making the tea, she was worse than useless. The third girl in the Department, the copy typist, was, on the other hand, excellent, could decipher Pringle's handwriting even when he himself was stumped by it, and would have the perfectly typed draft back to him in minutes.

He got the overnight telegrams and the original version and laid them out in front of him. He composed a rather testy first paragraph. Gilbert Winter would not like it but it would give him his views. Winter would substitute something more sedate, more precise, more appeasing.

One of the two telephones on the desk rang. An idiotic call from someone in Trade Policy Department asking for comments on a paper on Strategic Goods Embargoes to which he had replied weeks before. He told him where to find it and slammed the phone down. In the process he had lost the thread of the argument he had decided on, and had to start all over again.

Ten o'clock and Lawrence who shared his office, came in noisily. The trouble was that though Pringle found him agreeable enough, he considered him dim. He was on a desk dealing with a subject that neither interested him nor kept him busy enough to get off Pringle's back. He talked about the play he had seen the previous night—some conventionally praised pop-culture spectacular. Wonderful, he said. Pringle grunted non-committally. He had seen it on the first night. Lawrence went on to describe a party he had gone to. Pringle cut him short too abruptly telling him he had a rush job on. Lawrence took it sulkily and went around banging the steel doors of his combination cupboard for the next few minutes. Then he settled down to his hobby, a half-hour chat with his stockbroker about his portfolio. Pringle always felt the stockbroker must be pretty poor at his job or equally underemployed to be able to spare Lawrence the time. Only much later did he discover how enormously wealthy Lawrence was. He paid him more attention from then on, not through any hope of reward, but out of interest as to how someone he considered such a fool could be, and remain, so rich.

By ten-twenty he had finished the draft. He sprinted across the corridor to seek out the copy typist. She obligingly removed the work she was doing from her machine and began on it at once. At that moment the Head of the Department, Anderly, came in. It was his paper she had been working on and he protested. Pringle pointed out civilly that Anderly had his own PA. If she were off sick it was not Pringle's fault. Anderly complained that his stuff was just as urgent; Pringle responded that if he felt so strongly he should argue the toss with Gilbert Winter.

As Desk Officer, or First Secretary dealing with Britain's bilateral relations with the States on the political side, Pringle had Anderly as his boss, and he was a major irritation to him. Winter was the Under-Secretary. Normally, Desk Officers worked and submitted upwards through their Heads of Department. But personalities came into it; Winter disliked Anderly and felt he was an unnecessary cog in the wheel and had Pringle working directly to him. Anderly had objected; it weakened his authority, eroded his empire. He had had a confrontation with Winter and had threatened to take his complaint higher up. Winter had pacified him, told him that he, Anderly, was doing an excellent job, that there was no question of by-passing his authority, but just relieving the enormous pressures and work load under which he was so excellently working. Anderly left, mollified and flattered, and, though he realised he had lost the battle, did not pursue the matter again. But it hardly made the working relationship with Pringle a particularly happy one.

Anderly kept on about the urgency of his work. Pringle took five minutes to argue with him while the copy typist went battering on with his draft. Anderly, a thick-set Scot, had a distinct lack of any of the charm or veneer which most Foreign Office people acquire. They got it not because they were made or bred that way, as received opinion has it, but to protect themselves and their private lives from the constant round of social living which is one of the most insufferable, but unfortunately highly-valued, aspects of diplomatic life. He had come in from some industrial firm half way through his career, and the Civil Service Commission had, in Pringle's view, made one of their infrequent mistakes in passing him. He was a barrack-room lawyer with a great ability to rub both colleagues and foreigners the wrong way without appearing to notice. A difficult man to post, as Personnel Department would say, Anderly had come in full of zeal and misdirected energy. If he had, like his subordinate, been bright or his judgement sound, he would have been forgiven, for the Office has a large proportion of eccentrics. But he was neither. Pringle tended to ignore him as best as he could, but it was difficult. He usually tried to let his remarks pass him by but on this occasion he hammered back at him, told Anderly more or less to his face that he was getting in his way, that he, Pringle had real work to do. The copy typist pressed on with the draft; but Pringle was aware that the tea maker and a passing messenger had paused in their work in fascinated attention. Anderly exploded; Pringle was about to respond equally forcefully and they were poised on the brink of a first-class scene, when the copy typist ripped the finished draft from her machine, thrust it into Pringle's hands, giggled "Just made it," with a purposeful look at the office wall clock, and held the office door open for him. Pringle turned away from Anderly, beamed at the girl and left. A wonderful girl, hideous, a figure like a rake, but with a heart of gold. He never could remember her name, but he must take care to thank her. Winter would make him apologise to Anderly, but thanks to the girl, it was still at the apologisable stage. A moment or two more and he would have been moved to some other job, and that would have been a pity. Whoever had been to blame, Personnel would have thought a row most improper and, for face-saving and authority reasons, Anderly would not be the one to move. Not that with Anderly's record it would have done Pringle lasting harm but....

He went down the one flight, along the corridor and into Winter's room. Never knock on a door in the Foreign

Office; he remembered being told that when he first joined. If you go in and find you are disturbing someone, withdraw quietly. A knock is intrinsically much more disturbing.

The Legal Adviser was already there. Pringle sighed inwardly; it was going to be a lengthy and tedious business and he decided that he'd done enough work for one morning. He'd let the draft speak for itself; Winter and the lawyer could tear it to bits if they wanted to. He settled back in an armchair, nursing the cup of tepid coffee that Winter's PA had thoughtfully provided. It didn't work. Pride of authorship died hard and within five minutes he was defending his draft tooth and nail.

Two hours later he was feeling better pleased. The draft had gone through all the hoops and was now in the Private Office awaiting the Secretary of State's arrival from Scotland for the final initial before despatch. He had even fitted in a quick, not terribly well received, apology to Anderly. He went in and gushed out all about the rush he'd been in; how he'd been too hasty; he hoped he would forgive him. Anderly muttered something which would have been tactless had Pringle cared, about his having put his bad manners down to the strain of Pringle's recently dissolved marriage. He muttered "Yes, I suppose ..." and then left the room rapidly before Anderly could add something that might put the clock back. Pringle flashed a grateful smile at the shorthand typist who blushed and went on hammering with increased vigour at her machine.

Back in his office, Lawrence looked up and beamed "Panic over?"

"For an hour or two."

"Couple of messages while you were out." Lawrence thumbed leisurely through the buff Confidential file in front of him. Pringle could see the title. It read: 'Draft Convention on the Protection of the Blue Whale.' Poor old blue whale, if its extinction were to be prevented by the efforts of Lawrence.

"Library wants you. And some bird called Helen who's ringing back."

"Who in Library?"

"I scribbled a name somewhere." Eventually he found a scrap of paper and passed it across. Pringle picked up the receiver and asked for a Cornwall House number. The voice at the other end introduced itself. He was a man Pringle had met on a course somewhere.

"Sorry to trouble you. Small chore. Sending you a bundle of papers; end of the war; 'forty-five, 'forty-six. Could you just shuffle through them and see there's nothing that's going to cause libel actions and so on? You know the form." As he spoke, a diminutive messenger staggered through the door carrying three black despatch boxes.

"They've arrived," Pringle said, "but you've got the wrong man."

"No. Weren't you told? The Librarian spoke to Mr Anderly."

"What are they about?"

"Germany. Third party contacts with the Military Government, Neo-Nazi organisations, and so on."

"Wrong department. This is American Department. Anyway I thought all these papers were released ages ago and sent to the Public Record Office."

"They were. Trouble is now we're in rather a rush. These extra papers turned up. Very simple. They were hidden behind a pile of bound State Papers in a cupboard everyone thought was empty. Bit of a fuss. They're all marked for release, but we'd like you to go through them."

"There's a department that does that. The ... er ... what d'you call it? Or get the German Desk Officer."

"He's on overtime on the FRG/GDR Treaty. The boys that usually do this are busy on the translation work for the EEC debate. They were drafted in without as much as a by-your-leave. You probably saw the PM promise to lay the authoritative translations before the House before the end of the month."

"So why me?"

"You've passed the Higher Exam. Personnel gave us a list. It's pretty involved German."

"So have dozens of..."

"Anderly said."

"Oh to hell with Anderly. OK. When I've got time." Pringle made to put the phone down.

"Hang on. This week it has to be."

"Why the bloody..." Lawrence at the desk opposite him was looking across with some surprise. He always took Pringle for a testy, difficult colleague, but his language on the telephone was sharp for twelve forty-five in the Foreign and Commonwealth Office.

"Dr Pickforth at Sussex University is following something up. He asked for various references and we said we had no trace of them. He was adamant, and said he knew these papers existed."

"And these are...?"

"Yes. We did an enormous search and unfortunately found them. Trouble is, one of our clerks rang him up and told him we had traced them. Now he's in a hurry and thinks we're holding something back. Threatening to get some MP friend to put down a PQ. Administrative hiccough. Glad you can help."

"And I'm the only bloody German speaker in the ... What are we running? This isn't the Inland Revenue. What happened to that crash German language laboratory scheme? I thought we were into Europe..."

"Hold on. Hold on. Sorry: should have said a lot of the stuff's in Serbo-Croat too. You know both. The combination of both languages limits us a bit more and ... you volunteered you know. Anderly said you'd be happy to help."

Pause, two, three. "OK," Pringle said wearily and put the phone down. It wasn't Library's fault. He felt like going and withdrawing his apology. That tedious git. He looked at the three boxes, got up, picked them up one by one for they were heavy, and put them unopened at the bottom of his cupboard. He'd watched Lawrence pack up for lunch five minutes earlier. He'd had enough. He rang a friend in News Department. He was free too. A lengthy and hospitable lunch at the Travellers' was called for. The United States, Gilbert Winter, Anderly and the German files could wait an hour or two. As he left the room Pringle's phone was ringing. He let it ring, forgetting who else had rung that morning.

CHAPTER FIVE

Berlin, November 1945

PRIORITY HAD BEEN given to clearing the streets of rubble. Bulldozed clear through the huge mounds of desolation, they were the only signs of a return to life. Almost empty, they were littered by only an occasional figure hurrying along on some permitted errand, eager to escape back to its underground refuge. It was strange that life still seemed to survive under the grey dust that had settled over everything.

From a hole underneath one of the anonymous piles of rubble and broken glass a grimy child appeared pulling behind it a broken scooter. He left it at the entrance to the hole and started playing with some of the rubble. He built himself a little house of brick topped with a jagged piece of broken glass, a bright airy house; the child would not know one like it for many years to come. There was no wood in his tiny construction, for all the remnants of doors and window frames had been dragged away by the remaining inhabitants of Berlin as fuel for cooking and heating. The child played there happily until it was almost dusk. He started coughing either from the dust or from the onset of tuberculosis, and a woman's voice called him back into his cellar.

At that moment a man appeared at the end of what had once been a neat tree-lined street. Wilhelm Schenker had known Berlin well but he was to be forgiven for not knowing it in the last months of 1945. By and large the streets ran where they had always done, but there were few landmarks, the street signs were buried with everything else, the shells of buildings that were still standing had lost most of their features, with blackened empty window frames, and everywhere the grey dust. He hesitated, then turned up a side street towards the Tiergarten. What had once been a pleasant place to walk was now a graveyard of treestumps, the wood taken like everything else that burned. Only a few incongruous statues remained, towering above the remnants of the past.

The man stopped at a corner and pulled back into the shadow cast by the wall of a building as a jeep with four soldiers in it drove past on patrol. He was not worried now that he was in Berlin again. His papers were in good order. They showed that he was one of those who had fought the Nazis, had been persecuted by them. He had passed through many checkpoints, but it was always better to be on the safe side.

He saw at last what he was looking for: an arched gateway with a damaged coat of arms above it stood as the entrance to the courtyard of a large prosperous house. But of the house and the courtyard only the arch remained. He passed through it and, as he did so, a piece of masonry crashed on to the path behind him. At the noise, a woman's face appeared like a rat among a pile of rubble, the entrance to her underground refuge. She looked at the man curiously, then, satisfied that he seemed to offer no danger, she disappeared. Schenker called after her. She reappeared. He gave a man's name. Where was he, he asked? The woman shrugged, said nothing and made to disappear again. The man moved forward and seized her roughly by the arm, repeating his question. She looked at him with puzzlement rather than fear. Her capacity to fear had been overspent a hundred times in the past year.

"He is dead, I suppose, like them all."

"Why do you suppose that? He was alive till the end." There was no need to say what end the stranger was talking about.

"Who are you? I know nothing, nothing. Perhaps he is

in prison awaiting trial. Why don't you ask the British? They have their lists. They can be helpful if you're clean."

"Were you here on the last nights?"

"And what if I was?" The woman pulled herself away and drew back towards the door to the cellar.

"Did he get out? Did he get away?"

Suddenly her voice changed in pitch and intensity. "Oh yes. He got out from here all right, days before, and a whole lorryload of stuff with him. But where he got to, God knows. There are some that hope it wasn't far. He killed for the lorry, he killed for the petrol and he left his wife and children behind when he went." The woman spat in the dust. In the old days she would never have done such a thing, but there was no place for manners now.

"How d'you know?"

"The bastard was my husband."

There was a pause, but neither of them moved. "Why do you want him?" she asked after some moments. "Who are you?"

"My business."

"I know," she said with something resembling a smile. "It's not him you want, it's what he's got. That's it isn't it? Those boxes he had, those little heavy boxes that came from the Bank strongroom. Well he took them with him anyway."

"Where?"

"I tell you I don't know."

"But perhaps?"

"What will you do when you find him?"

"That depends."

"Pull the trigger once more for me." The woman turned away and the man made to leave. He had drawn a blank. He would have to start all over again. But then the woman called from her hole, "Brother's house, outside Hamburg. Try there. The British Zone would be safer he always said

Try Koblenzerstrasse number a hundred and nine; a big house with a mock gothic tower. And if you find him pull the trigger once for me."

The man's shoes crunched on the broken glass as he walked away into the night.

Foreign and Commonwealth Office, London, S.W.1

The bottle of Travellers' Club Burgundy which Pringle shared with his News Department colleague made him far from energetic, but they did a brisk tour round St James's Park afterwards and he ended up feeling reasonably alert. There was a touch of early frost in the air, the fallen leaves crackled underfoot, the ducks swam thickly over the lake, and London was as bracing as it occasionally can be in early November. He came back into the Office in a rather better frame of mind and made a determined set at the pile of papers and files which had been accumulating in his trays.

Nearly every one of them pointed to the fact that Anglo-American relations were going through a bad patch and he was up to his eyes in work, though he was far from sure where it was all leading. How long ago was it now since the intelligence reports of serious moves inside the United States Administration to pull out of NATO had first come in? It was only a few weeks ago that he had had a hand in drafting the secret Planning Staff Paper; he had it in front of him now, to update some of the annexes. The paper, with a bluntness unusual in the Office, pointed to the tensions and drew some pretty gloomy conclusions. It began by arguing that camouflaged by Watergate, by the aftermath of the Middle East War and by the growing energy crisis, the pressures from certain sections of the US governmental machine to pursue a basically 'America First' line were understandable. What had the Europeans shown recently except bickering and ingratitude for American diplomatic efforts? Internal problems they had in sufficient quantity to keep everyone occupied. Why waste the American Secretary of State's qualities settling other people's problems when there were plenty on the home front? The Administration needed a good clean-up, and a total US military and political disengagement all round the globe, though it would cause an initial shock in World capitals, could only be of economic and political advantage to the United States and its people.

This was the argument. The silent majority were waiting for an occasion to become vocal. They needed a voice, a leader to direct them, to avoid the resultant noise sounding like a babble of folly. Most international observers thought they knew best. Wise men sat around, smiled a little and said that it was all talk. It could never happen. The present problems would run themselves out of steam; nothing more would be heard of demands for American isolationism, except from the usual extremists. America would remain America. It could never turn its back on the world again.

What the wise men in their clubs, the political commentators in the press and elsewhere did not realise, but what was pointed up in the Planning Paper, was how strong this growing isolationist lobby was, both inside and outside the Administration. Unlike most other lobbies in Washington, the danger of this group was that, as yet, it appeared to be operating without any popular appeals to the public, almost in secret, as if it knew that the silent majority would be with it when the time came. It was particularly dangerous because it was an informed group; the Planning Paper identified Senators, Congressmen, state servants and diplomats among its ranks. To these individuals, pulling every American serviceman back to the States was no folly, but enlightened self-interest. But as the Paper pointed out, what the group lacked was cohesion and leadership. It had lacked it until recently.

The relatively unknown Senator Dwight C. Mainfare had taken up the call. His name began appearing in reports with telling frequency. The British Embassy in Washington knew little about him beyond the briefest biography; they knew more about his *front man*, as they called him, his former Senate colleague and personal adviser, Mr Henry A. Middleton.

When one is a Senator in the United States of America it is a truism to say that one has arrived. Senator Henry A. Middleton certainly had done that. He emerged from almost total obscurity at the age of about thirty to pursue a highly successful decade of law studies, beginning modestly at a college that no one had heard of, and finishing up with a mass of doctorates and prizes from the Harvard Law School. He left two well-received books and a budding academic career in 1959 at the ripe age of forty-one, much older than most of his fellow students, but none the less vigorous for that. He shone in every way, and, as is the nature of things, was creamed off immediately by one of the top law partnerships in New York City. If his rise through the academic world had been sharp and successful, his law practice in the decade that followed was outstanding. A series of dull but profitable, then profitable and famous court cases in support of various large business firms paid off handsomely. On the back of these he entered politics with the same dedication and brilliance that he demonstrated in his chosen career. He moved out of New York to a provincial centre, where he seemed to have had an even better set of connections, successful cases and political victories, and with uncanny foresight, managed to leapfrog most of the normal stages in the political success process and was elected Senator on the unexpected death of the sitting tenant, at the age of forty-nine.

A big, handsome, blond man, with high cheek bones and a well-kept complexion. A fair athlete, though sometimes a poor loser on the tennis court, he had a stiff good humour and charm which produced him more acquaintances then friends, but very few known enemies, and none of them bitter in their opposition. His credentials were impeccable. He was not born in the States, he and his parents fled from Austria in the late 'thirties to escape—not the anti-Jewish troubles—he carefully explained that he was a Calvinist—but because his father had been too much a liberal-democrat for the politics of the time. There were no apparent scandals in his past, no early hidden vices nor present ones either. He married well into another legal family whose head died shortly after the marriage, thereby swelling the already swollen Middleton fortunes.

Article One, Section Three, Paragraph Three of the Constitution of the United States of America reads: "No person shall be a Senator who shall not have attained to the age of thirty years, and been nine years a citizen of the United States, and who shall not, when elected, be an inhabitant of that State for which he shall be chosen". There were no problems there either. Circumstance, connections, money, charm and great ability transformed Henry A. Middleton into Senator Henry A. Middleton overnight.

But one or two electoral periods later and things were drastically different. He was personally clean, everyone said so. But his local party was rotten to the core and he had not seen it; he had done nothing until, too late, he had learned what was amiss. Bribery, graft, prostitution, protection, corruption and tax evasion had flourished on a vast scale. Appointments and favours had been given widely in his name. Against the backcloth of his party sweeping the board in nearly every other state, this man, branded as honest but naïve, was swept from power. That his electorate rapidly became sorry that they had not kept their trust and had instead elected an unprincipled and dishonest fool, was neither here nor there. Middleton was on the political rubbish dump. Or was he?

Sometime in the Summer of 1973 he began appearing as the spokesman for the 'Mainfarers' as the America-first group was called. By the autumn, largely due to him, it was becoming clear what the group aims were. It was not just a call for disengagement in Europe; there was more to it than that. The Washington Embassy went as far as to define it as being anti-European, with the slings particularly directed, for no clear reason, at Britain.

But Britain was not alone in noting this development with some concern. While they found that attacks on their Irish policies were starting to emanate from the Mainfarers as well, the Federal German Government found itself the subject of increasing criticism for its Ostpolitik. Informal talks about these developments were held with Bonn, but while the Mainfarers were trespassing on both German and British internal affairs, both decided to sit it out, say nothing, and hope that this particular irritation to US-European relations would go away. And as the public and the media in both the United States and in Europe paid little attention to the Mainfarers since they lacked the secret information available to governments, there were no external pressures on the Foreign Office to take any urgent action. In October, the public realised that something was amiss within the Administration, quite apart from Watergate. There were one or two strange resignations in top Washington circles; there were reports of political alliances being made between traditionally incompatible groups. The press speculated, put most of it down in the end to personal rather than political differences, and after a few days the fuss died down.

Pringle's role was to analyse rather than act, to keep his diplomatic and political superiors briefed on the state of play, and to work out contingency plans, in case the US Administration decided to give in to one of the many internal pressures on it and agree to a certain limited pull out. It might also be a useful gambit for them at the current stage of their Strategic Arms Limitation talks with the Russians.

There was no doubt that if the Mainfarers had their way, the withdrawal of the American presence from Europe would be warmly welcomed in many quarters in the Continent itself; jubilant demonstrations would take place in the streets of Paris and London. Further East, the increasingly outward-going men of the Kremlin would watch with restrained interest. The Planning Staff analysis was that they would not do anything, since they would see that any move by them might halt a process which well suited them. Besides, they were too busy watching over their shoulders the equally turbulent events in Peking.

The work that Kissinger and Nixon had begun of changing the strategy of American Foreign Policy from the old Acheson-Dulles line of encouraging close alliances and power blocks, towards a flexible balance of power relying on shifting *ad hoc* combinations of interest, was being threatened by these pressures for a military and political retreat from the world. But that on its own would be liveable with. A United Europe was strong enough to stand on its own feet. If, for internal reasons, the President did give in, why worry? One answer was that with the single-minded naïvety of the politically inexperienced, Senator Mainfare and his backwoodsmen followers were, in addition, trying to defeat the combined advice of the State Department, the Pentagon, the CIA and the Department of Commerce, and were urging an all-out trade war. According to intelligence reports most senior officials and diplomats were standing in the way of what they considered to be such a suicidal policy. But some of the more important of these men were either being dismissed or moved to less central functions. In one or two crucial posts, the new appointees were Mainfare supporters or sympathisers. Bit by bit policies formulated by the Department of Commerce, in particular, were undergoing significant change.

At the end of October the Foreign Office first picked up information that the Mainfarers were being backed by two of the largest American conglomerates. In return for their support they were promised discriminatory policies, tax concessions, and high protective tariff walls of their choosing. There was evidence to suggest that large sums of money had been given or promised by these two enterprises. And still the alert pressmen in Washington and London were silent; they were too occupied by Watergate.

The Planning Staff paper ended on an inconclusive note: it was hard to estimate the real extent of the Mainfare threat; there was some way to go yet before Britain needed to get worried; there would be no sudden declaration of war, but pressures on a badly troubled Administration might suddenly bring success for the isolationists. Nothing formal would be said; no explanations or apologies or excuses would be forthcoming. People had always talked about the possibility of a trade war with the United States. There had been similar fears in the past, but while few thought the dangers to be anything but minimal at present, everyone who had worked on the Planning Paper was agreed on one thing: if the Common Market countries had, at some future time, to resort to retaliatory measures, then the economic wars of the past would be as nothing compared to the prospect of this all-out European-American trading confrontation.

Though Anderly was far from gracious about it, Pringle took Friday the ninth off, and went up to Scotland for a long weekend, returning by overnight sleeper to Kings Cross on the Sunday night. At six-fifty on a Monday morning in November, London, particularly north London, is a dreary place. The weekend's litter had yet to be cleared away; the only other people who seemed to be travelling were soldiers. It brought back memories of National Service, train journeys always at night, waiting interminably for connections at Newcastle, Carlisle or Duisburg.

A taxi back to his flat and he pushed his way in over the small pile of letters, advertising material and newspapers that had accumulated since the previous Friday. He went through to the kitchen and put on a kettle for coffee. Then he started to run a bath. The phone rang. He disliked telephone calls before seven or after eleven at night. Bad tidings or wrong numbers. It was the Resident Clerk at the Office. He knew him.

"What the hell, Richard? It's just gone seven."

"Could you come in at once please?"

"Oh to hell, I've just come down from Scotland on the sleeper. Can't you ring Anderly?"

"Why Anderly?" The Resident Clerk was polite.

"Anderly, my boss, lad. Wakey wakey. American Department. Look, I'm dead tired, need a shave and I've got the bath running, but I'll ring him if you like and get him to talk to you."

"You're not the only one tired. I haven't slept since suddenly everyone's discovered there's an oil shortage. But Anderly isn't involved. You've got some papers; you're sitting on some files and they can't get into your cupboard to get at them. You're needed in the Office now." The Resident Clerk put the phone down.

Pringle was determined. He took his coffee to his bath, but both were too hot. He had forgotten the Library files. They had been sleeping a long time; what was the rush suddenly on a Monday morning? Twenty-five years collecting dust and only a week at the bottom of his cupboard.

Why the fuss? They could wait the couple of hours till he got in.

But doubt and discipline set in in equal doses. If the Resident Clerk was ringing at this hour ... He left coffee and bath, had a rapid shave, and went in, pushing his mail into his briefcase on his way.

CHAPTER SIX

Foreign and Commonwealth Office, London, S.W.1

A MAN WAS waiting in his office. He was small, with a thin mournful face and fair-to-grey hair plastered down on top of his head with haircream. He did not give his name, but explained, in sorrow rather than anger, that he had been hanging about for an hour and a half, waiting for Pringle to turn up. It was now quarter past eight; they had to see one of the library files urgently. He did not say who 'they' were but Pringle supposed it must be a security matter, a guilty secret out of someone's past, which was not to be released to Dr Pickforth and the general public.

As he dialled the combination lock of his cupboard, Pringle was lectured to by the little man on the sins of not ensuring that other people in his department knew the code number. He promised to stick faithfully to the rules in future. It made Pringle nervous and he got the combination wrong twice before it would open, then had to find the key for the three despatch boxes, which also took some time, since it was hidden away at the bottom of one of his trays. The man waited in total silence; despite that, Pringle was aware that underneath his placid exterior the man was seething at his dilatoriness.

He found the key, discovered the file the man wanted in the last box he opened and handed it over. It was in a battered green cardboard cover and had the words *Neo-Nazis: Miscellaneous*, inked in on the front. The man thumbed through it rapidly and then, unprofessionally, when he found the paper he was looking for, he simply ripped it out, folded it and put it away in an inside pocket. Then he handed Pringle the file back.

"Thank you for coming in," he said softly.

"Oh, not at all. Not at all." Pringle echoed sarcastically. "Any time. I like it. Particularly after a sleepless night on a train. And don't bother telling me what it's all about." But the man had left the room by the time he had finished speaking.

Pringle decided to stay and catch up with his work. What was a missed breakfast in a good cause? Before he settled down, however, he went across to a bookcase and took out a copy of *Who's Who*. The name Geoffrey Benner, which he had seen at the top of the minute paper his visitor had ripped from the file, struck a chord. It was a 1970 edition of *Who's Who*, but it was sufficient to remind him who Benner was today.

He spent the next two hours working steadily through the pile of papers in his tray. Despatches, telegrams, memoranda; there were always crises in the Office. Attention moved from one to another with polished ease. The Middle East War which had erupted on October the sixth had given way to an uneasy peace; now everyone was worried about oil supplies. People concerned with United States affairs were reading the small print on Watergate in the aftermath of the President handing some of the tapes over to Judge Sirica on the twenty-second of the month. The President had mixed oil and Watergate in his nationwide television address on the evening of the seventh of November, and ended by rejecting calls for his resignation. Special Prosecutors and Attorney Generals were resigning or being dismissed right, left and centre, and the Vice Presidential Candidate, Mr Gerald Ford, was undergoing closer scrutiny than any of his predecessors. In Britain, Royal Wedding bells drowned the background of potential economic catastrophe, which the prophets of gloom claimed as heralding the end of things as we knew them.

The Washington Embassy kept sending back the latest intelligence on the Mainfarers' activities, but played the matter down. The telegrams from other posts made no mention of any incipient crisis in United States relations with Western Europe. The strands in the web of Anglo-American relations had been fragile for years like the diplomatic and political ties of the 'Special Relationship' of Harold MacMillan and others. In real terms, this relationship had amounted to little, especially when it came to a crisis with national interests at stake; then each side had consulted the other only when it had something to gain and when it had suited them to do so. When it did not, as over the Middle-East policies of the Americans or the European policies of the British, each had long gone its own way; there was nothing very special about that. Again, on the possibilities of American military withdrawal, while a few years earlier the European states would have looked anxiously eastward at any such potential development, the Mutual and Balanced Force Reduction talks in Vienna and elsewhere meant that nowadays it was almost unthinkable that the Russians or their allies would take any advantage from such a withdrawal and cross the demarkation lines of the Continent.

To Pringle, more interesting than the subject matter itself, were the methods, the mechanics of negotiation. It was pure diplomacy, one of the reasons why he had joined the Office, this detailed, often frustrating negotiation first with Britain's European partners, then with the Americans, along lines which had been worked out earlier between the Foreign Office and the civil servants of Whitehall. For foreign policy was never left to the Foreign and Commonwealth Office alone, and the Treasury, the Bank of England and the Department of Trade and Industry all had their views, since, in the eyes of the home civil servants, diplomats were suspect, a race apart, thinking they alone knew best when it came to dealing with 'the foreigner'.

About ten-thirty, Anderly sent for Pringle and asked how he was getting on with weeding the Library files. He blew his top, and Anderly retreated. But the respite did not last long. The man from the Foreign Office Library also rang to ask if he had finished; could he please send them straight back?

"I'll send them back all right, but I warn you I haven't touched them."

"Oh my God, Dr Pickforth from Sussex has been on to us again. We're in for a lot of trouble."

Pringle explained as coolly as he could. He had work to do for the department and that came first. Take it or leave it. No question of getting round to them sooner, he said confidently.

The man from the Library was non-committal, apologised for bothering him, said he hadn't realised how pressed he was, said he would see what else he could arrange. At twelve Pringle was summoned to see Winter and told to deal with the files, crisis or no crisis. Winter said he had told them where to go when they first asked him, but had been overruled.

Pringle was damned if he was going to waste the rest of the day. He sent a secretary out to get some sandwiches, phoned a friend he arranged to meet for lunch and called it off, then settled down to the files, in a highly irritated frame of mind. But it did not last long and he rapidly became absorbed in the past.

Some of the documents were fascinating. Winter would approve of the style of minuting; much more coherent, more elegant, written for posterity. Today's minuting was blunt and to the point, often humorous if not coarse. Emotive adjectives were deleted. It would be wrong to upset the balance of the argument by introducing feeling or emotion. In thirty years' time, American PhD students, or Soviet PhD students would have a simpler, less elevated task but perhaps by then some form of *newspeak* would be the fashion and all this clever casualness would be as strange as that of the mid-forties.

The amount of Serbo-Croat needed was almost nil, and Pringle realised it had been used more as an argument to get him to do the work than anything else. But there was an amount of documentation in German; highly classified High Command papers which had come to light in the immediate aftermath of the War and had been given some brief study then. Whatever the dating on the original German papers, the whole series of files were in a category dealing with Neo-Nazi movements in the first post-war months. The Allied Military Government had been worried about the threat and the papers concerned a number of named individuals round whom much of this activity had operated. One name that kept appearing in the papers was that of a man called Wilhelm Schenker, who had had a function in the Führerbunker as an aide to Hitler himself. He had escaped from Berlin at the end of the war and had disappeared, no one knew where. Then he had re-emerged and there were reports of his having travelled widely round the Allied Sectors of Germany on forged papers, and having made contact with a number of minor figures with Nazi pasts. From the files there was almost nothing to go on as to why he should have been considered so important, though there was a hint that large sums of money had changed hands. A letter between two unidentified Germans which had been intercepted by the Military Authorities referred to Schenker's role as an international linkman and financial courier with expatriate Nazis in South America. This was confirmed in a minute from a British diplomat writing from Berlin in July, 1946. There was no date or evidence to support this report, but there was a cross reference to a paper on another of the file series. Pringle searched for it, but it was missing. Then he saw the tell-tale screw of paper round the string Treasury tag that bound the whole file together, and thought about the little man who had torn one single minute from his file.

The ink on the photocopy had faded badly, the handwriting was uneven and he had to struggle to make sense of it, but the story the anonymous letter-writer told indicated that Schenker had on at least one occasion used violence to get hold of Third Reich funds which had disappeared in the aftermath of the war.

He came with a list and eventually found ten of us to help him. Two or three came most unwillingly; I could not blame them for they had had enough of war and death, and even though the grip of the British Military Authorities was far from complete in the Hamburg area, the penalties for being caught would have been severe.

It was a large house with a monstrous gothic tower, set well back from the road. The rambling overgrown garden had been neglected for years but the house itself was in better condition than most others in the area. The windows were all complete, and damage to the roof had been repaired. Schenker had been efficient in his enquiries; the man we were after had already established a flourishing black market operation and yet he was in full favour with the Military Authorities. This made us angry. Schenker had christened him The Snake.

We approached the house at two o'clock in the morning, four at the back, four at the front and the other three to watch the side windows. There was a full moon and that helped. We had plenty of time, for the nearest soldiers were billeted in a school on the outskirts of the town three kilometres away. Schenker had found us weapons easily enough; we were to abandon them at the house once it was over.

I rang the bell. A dog barked somewhere and The Snake came down and opened the door a fraction. He had it on a chain. I caught a glimpse of a woman in a dressing-gown looking out nervously from behind him. I stood on my own at the door; the others were out of sight.

"*What do you want?*"
"*I have a message for you.*"
"*From whom?*"
"*From Berlin.*"
"*Why do you come at this time of night?*"
"*Some of us cannot travel by day. I have come a long way and it is cold.*"

The Snake hesitated. The little I could see of him suggested that the name we had given him was appropriate. He was tall and thin, and his gaunt face had a greenish tinge in the hall light. The door closed and I heard whispers. When it opened again he had released the chain. He stood there, a raincoat wrapped round his pyjamas, and he had a pistol in his hand. I was expecting that, for only a fool would have opened up in such circumstances without protection.

As the door opened, Schenker, who was waiting with a torch, flashed a message to the men at the rear of the house. As planned, one of them hammered on the rear door. The Snake turned at the sound and I knocked him out with my life preserver. It was simple.

By the time he came round we had locked the woman in a cupboard and had searched the house without success. He began by saying that he did not have the gold, that it was still in Berlin. We tied him up then and it took us precisely forty minutes to get him to break. One of the colleagues knew the techniques; he used two electric wires connected to a wall socket, but claimed he could have had just as much effect with a cigarette butt. I did not like to watch and waited outside trying not to listen to the screams.

Then he showed us: he had walled up a cupboard with brick, with his own hands. He had plastered and painted it over and then he had soiled the paintwork to make it blend in with the rest of the room. We would have had to destroy the whole house before we had found the gold.

We carried the boxes out to the lorry, leaving The Snake tied up in his chair. As we were about to leave, Schenker told us to wait and went back into the house. I heard two shots.

"Was that necessary?" I asked him later.

"It was necessary. One shot was necessary. The other was a present from his wife."

Pringle had a long lunch on Friday the twenty-third with Miller from Security Department. He knew him of old; they had been to a lot of NATO meetings in Brussels together. He was a big man of about forty-five with a heavy pleasant face and a shock of fair curly hair twenty years too young for him. He looked as if he had played lock in many a rugby scrum, but his bluff, hearty exterior and jolly-good-old-boy laugh concealed, as Pringle had quickly learned, an able intellect with reserves of cunning and an ability to make fools of those conceited enough to consider they had summed him up. He had the great quality of being able to lead people into carefully formulated traps of his own construction, to expose their lack of ability, and then to reveal all with the charm and giggles of a sixth form public schoolboy, to the delight of anyone listening. They agreed to meet at the Travellers'.

Any new entrant to diplomacy rapidly realises how unrelated is practice and popular reputation in the workings of the Diplomatic Service. Old images die hard and, except in the public mind, bowler hats and pinstripes have long been left for chartered accountants and bankers to wear. Bright shirts and loud ties go with the real personality of the Office, which can be claimed to average out at left-of-centre liberalism. When the man with the beard at the Stockwell party had suggested that Pringle was slumming it by going south of the river, he was out of date. Many of his colleagues lived in unfashionable areas though there was still a lurking minority who were decidedly old school, who might not know where Stockwell was. It was true, however, that for nearly all of them there were still some occasional upper-echelon diversions, and the use of the Travellers' was one of them.

At five to one he left the Foreign Office by the gate opposite Number Ten, turned down the steps towards St James's Park, past the high wall of the Prime Minister's garden and strolled possessively across the triangle of grass known as the Foreign Office Green. Over the road and through the Park, past the pelicans, the Guards' War Memorial with the public conveniences behind it, up and across the Mall to the Duke of York Steps. On a wall there, before Carlton House Terrace was renovated and re-painted, someone had scribbled a piece of high class graffiti: "Do not adjust your mind, there is a fault in reality". He thought of it every time he went that way. Past the Atheneum with its Bishops, Lords, beautiful rooms and public school food he turned the corner into Pall Mall, up the steps and in through the arrogantly anonymous door of the Travellers' Club, and joined Miller at a common table for sausage and mash and a piece of Stilton, with a glass of passable wine. An advantage of the Travellers' was that, if the mood took him, there was always someone to talk to, always others from the Office or from some of the more select nearby Embassies mingling with travellers, adventurers and would-be John Buchan heroes of the world. A disadvantage, if he were not in the mood, was that there was always someone to talk to him, and anonymity was impossible. But he had the choice, that upper-class freedom of choice as to whether he wanted to dine there or not.

After lunch he bought Miller a cognac in the library. They were on the favourite subject of younger diplomats, the perennial question of whether they would be better off in the outside world, in business where responsibility was backed by financial rewards for success and penalties for failure. How secure by comparison the closed society of a diplomatic career, where decisions were joint, where bad advice or faulty decisions were taken by committee and the public responsibility at the end was the Minister's. Unless a diplomat took bribes, which was unknown except for the well publicised motives of espionage, his decisions were decisions to formulate decisions, drafts of possible best courses of action in any given set of circumstances. Others amended or changed or approved them further up the tree. Occasionally an Ambassador, remote from the Foreign Office, made some false move, proffered poor advice which led to political or economic chaos—the odd international run on the pound, the unforeseen war. Even if the blame was eventually fixed on him and he was not able to justify his advice after the event he would still not have his pay docked, would not suffer a cut in his *frais*—those special allowances an Ambassador gets to keep the flag flying at Queen's Birthday Parties and the like—but his next posting would be to some quieter, even remoter place with only the reports on his file as his reward, rather than the bankruptcy court which would be his due in the commercial world.

They turned to the other favourite subject and reminisced; it occurred to Pringle that if he could do it so well at thirty-five what would he be like at sixty? He was always worried by incipient signs of burning himself out, a hallowed Foreign Service phrase for those many individuals who had ability once, but who had hammered about the globe for so many years that by the time they reached their late forties they had had too many cocktail parties, too many heavy dinners, too many boring receptions and had given up or worn themselves out. The Foreign Service had no more than its fair share of burnt out cases, but the Graham Greene character, discreetly debauched with years in the tropics and access to years of duty-free scotch to his credit, is in every Embassy.

At quarter to three they looked at their watches and ordered another round. They turned back to the benefits of their chosen profession, reassuring each other of its merits. Miller told him about a recruiting lecture he had given to students when he was in Personnel. He had talked about late night working in inhospitable posts, about the mundanities of the work as well as the bright spots where one saw ones work interpreted by journalists and translated to the front page of *The Times*. He had used the phrase about diplomats being the oil that made international relations work. Someone at the back of the lecture hall who had been heckling throughout and appeared to be in opposition to the Civil Service as an institution, bellowed out—"oily and well-oiled"—Terry had had to pause for a while to let the giggles subside. He then suggested that the man had the sort of quick wit the Service needed; could he come and see him afterwards? Laughter all round.

They broke off after that, left the Club and walked slowly back towards the Office. On the way they talked about responsibility. A popular view was that no really moral man could remain in a Service doing a job where as Governments changed, he must object to at least some of the policies being pursued. Pringle had come to terms with this on a number of issues. He could resign if the principle was strong enough, but he had always persuaded himself that it was wiser to stay in and work to change the policy. It happened often enough when a new Government came to power that policies expressed while in opposition were out of keeping with the influences and circumstances of the realities of power. But so often these so-called realities were the result of how the civil servants presented them.

"Talking about responsibility," Miller said as they parted company, "I'm sorry I had to get you in early the other day. We had to get a paper from one of those files you are working on."

"It was your man was it? Well he just ripped the paper out," Pringle said. "Hardly routine registry practice."

"Hardly a routine paper. It was a photostat of a document. We thought there was only one copy of it—a list of those British who collaborated with the Nazis."

"Like Sir Geoffrey Benner?"

Miller looked at him sharply. "Like him. But there were others, many of them dead; a few are still around and we don't want to stir things up again and embarrass people unless we have to. The leadership in successive Labour and Conservative Governments has consistently agreed to that. One copy for posterity but that's enough.

"And the same goes for Sir Geoffrey Benner?" Pringle asked.

"For the moment, the same goes for him."

CHAPTER SEVEN

Herr Walter von Sattendorf, Auswärtiges Amt, Bonn

HIS WIFE AND two-year-old son were with his parents-in-law at their genuine Bavarian schloss for a brief family reunion before they moved to London. As usual when he was by himself, he had a frugal breakfast: slightly stale brown bread with the taste of caraway seed, unsalted butter, but joy of joys, Cooper's Old English Marmalade, which he had acquired through a friend in the British Embassy in return for some rather special Ahr Auslese to which he had access. The reheated black coffee spoiled the effect, bringing back the bitter taste of the ersatz brew of his childhood.

Walter von Sattendorf carefully washed up the plate, the cup and saucer, the knife and the spoon, leaving them to dry in the rack by the sink. Nearly everything else was packed. He poured the remainder of the coffee down the drain; it would not stand another day. The breadknife was clean and he replaced it in the drawer. The bread he wrapped in the silver foil and put it in the 'fridge. He brushed and swilled away the breadcrumbs from the chopping board down the drain, turned off the taps, switched out the kitchen light and went into the hall of their neat and, as he said himself, characterless small house in Muffendorferstrasse, Bad Godesberg, the residential suburb of Bonn. He'd be glad to leave it, get back to living in a proper city again.

Coat, gloves and scarf, because there was snow in the air, he self-consciously allowed himself to put on the astrakhan hat he had bought during an official trip to Moscow last year. He was always at pains to dress correctly, a caution that in later life would develop into fussiness. This precision was also a part of his working life; he was irritated by untidiness and unclear thinking. Yet he himself, a thin dark man already balding who had a habit of peering over rather than through his fashionable heavy-rimmed spectacles, gave an impression of imprecision. He had a disconcerting habit of leaning towards the person he was with and opening his mouth in a way which suggested that he was about to say something weighty. Then he would pause, sit back and would not begin talking until his eye had fixed on a spot over the left shoulder of the listener, as if someone behind were being addressed.

Outside, he clicked the glass door shut behind him, and going through the garden gate, got into his silver-grey VW 1300 that had been parked in the street overnight. It started first time, and he backed out carefully into busy Muffendorferstrasse. Even he, at thirty-four, remembered it as a country lane before they built all the houses on the hill behind.

Down the hill, left past the Redoute and the town park, then right, left, and right again through the once attractive small village of Bad Godesberg and on to Friedrich Ebert Allée which blends bleakly in late November into the expanding town of Bonn. Just beyond the town sign he passed the ugly two-storey grey building that was the British Embassy, with its works canteen and car park beside it. Then into Bonn itself, a maze of 'Road Up' and 'Umleitung' signs, and to the Auswärtiges Amt where he worked. He parked his car in a side street where he had managed for the past few weeks to find a parking place without being fined, and walked towards the office itself. On the right was the smaller building where the Foreign Minister and some senior officials had their offices; on the left the main building. He showed his pass to the security guards, went up a few steps past the plaque in memory of the first post-war Federal Foreign Minister, to that one impressive feature of the building, the constantly moving chain of cages, the continuous elevator, to be carried up to the third floor office—or box, where he worked.

"Morgen, Klaus," he shouted to a colleague. He had served with him *en poste* in Washington. "Morgen, Walter," was shouted back. It wasn't that he knew Klaus particularly well, he knew many people better whom he continued to address as Herr or Frau so-and-so, but Washington which he had left nearly four years ago now, had broken down some of the formalities of the German way of life.

In his office he hung his coat and scarf on the coat hook behind the door. The fur hat he carefully laid on top of the cupboard. Fräulein Helmich came in with his trays of papers. Von Sattendorf had started noticing Fräulein Helmich, because she was going out of her way to ensure he did. Coffee came without his asking, she was always asking his advice in the most respectful way, and the shops of Bonn and Cologne were scoured for the shortest or most provocative skirts, the most plunging necklines. On occasion, when his wife, of whom he was very fond, was away for too long a period, it worked, and he felt his attention, so usually precise and singleminded, wandering towards large areas of upper leg and the infinite valley of her neckline.

"Guten Morgen, Fräulein Helmich." She smiled a deep-eyed smile and he quickly averted his eyes towards his tray. It was gratifyingly slim, for, in his present bachelor state and lacking any invitation which would have diverted him, he had worked on the previous evening to clear a whole backlog of work which had for too long clogged up his desk and which he wanted rid of before handing over to his successor. There were half a dozen small things to attend to in the wire mesh basket and the one larger problem which he had not dealt with the previous night because he had to consult the legal department of the Auswärtiges Amt plus the Ministry of Justice before formulating a policy proposal for his superiors.

As usual these files were in the series dealing with the problems of the North Atlantic Alliance. It had been his full-time job for several months now, ever since he had been taken off the work on EEC's Common Agricultural Policy to work on this new and increasingly baffling subject. He had watched it happen from a ringside seat, and it had been a fascinatingly inevitable process. The Atlantic Alliance had slept too long, and it now threatened to disintegrate with a rapidity that would take even the most expert and farseeing diplomatic observers by surprise. The European public were going to get an enormous shock one day when they wakened up to the fact that the Mainfarers had arrived, were a force to be reckoned with, and that things had changed fundamentally. But that was still to be grasped by all but a few in half a dozen Western capitals.

He had been to meetings in London, secret meetings of Ministers and officials to try to co-ordinate a joint contingency plan. So far there had been little success. The men behind Mainfare seemed hell-bent on isolationism whatever the cost. Unlike other opposition groups in Washington, they were on the inside, and it did not look as if there was anything the British, the Germans and the other West Europeans could do about it. Daily there were more reports from Washington of American planning directed at closing their doors on the rest of the World. A walk-out of NATO was now a distinct possibility. How often in the past would Germany have welcomed such American isolationism and withdrawal? But not now.

There would be many who would shrug their shoulders and say: So what? Why should the Europeans not stand entirely on their own feet once again. But there were more things at stake, and important people both in Europe and in the States recognised this. In the present troubled situation in Washington, Mainfare was an increasingly powerful man, and he claimed the silent majority would be silently behind him.

Fräulein Helmich came in noiselessly. He brought his eyes up as far as her cleavage, recognised it, paused a moment, and then looked at her enquiringly.

"Yes?"

She was carrying a cup of coffee. Instead of placing it in front of him, she came round behind him and placed it on the right of his writing pad. As she bent over to remove a paper from his out-tray, he felt the tips of her blouse brush against his shoulder. Despite the hour, a brief shiver of anticipation passed through him: there was nothing so attractive as a woman obviously available.

Her action completed, she answered him. "Dr Feuchtwanger wanted to see you as soon as you came in."

"He's quick off the mark."

"He has been in for an hour and a half already, Herr von Sattendorf."

"Prussian zeal."

"I believe he's of Austrian extraction, Sir."

"Yes, well ... what did he say it was about?"

"There's a telegram in from the Embassy in Washington. There are reports of a plan to cut their Military, Naval and Air Attaché staff in their Embassy here in Bonn. We are to be requested to do likewise and have ours out of Washington within the next three months."

"The next three months? What the hell? We always have lots of Attachés everywhere, it gives the soldiers something to do; even at the height of the Cold War we had ... Have we been singled out, do you know?

"Tell Feutchwanger I'm in." He looked at her and she jerked a quick smile at him. He watched her cleavage bounce seductively open and shut as she tripped out of the office.

Feuchtwanger, the Desk Officer for American-German bilateral relations, appeared about five minutes later, a large pile of green files bulging efficiently under his arm. He was a dark, severe little man with a scar down one cheek. Duelling at Heidelberg with a corps, or a genuine war wound? Most probably a car accident, von Sattendorf concluded.

"You've heard the latest nonsense?" Feuchtwanger spoke rapidly.

"What are they playing at? Yes, I've heard. Drawing in their horns with a vengeance. What beats me is why the Pentagon stands for it. What's happened to all these generals and so on who, we used to say, ran American foreign policy?"

"What's left of them are busy giving their energies and support to Mainfare on his internal Law and Order ticket." Feuchtwanger's face formed a look of distaste. "The news this morning has more reports of the shooting in Alabama. Ten blacks dead along with the Deputy Marshal they had as hostage."

"Hardly back-page news these days."

"And the front page story all about Pilkington. He used to be Counsellor at the British Embassy at the Hague. I knew him there. He seemed very attached to his wife then. The British always do these sex and drug scandals so much better than we continentals. It always appears to take them all so much by surprise."

"Who was this Pilkington supposed to be spying for?" von Sattendorf asked. He played with some paper clips on his desk as he spoke.

"Not sure. Something slightly unusual. Israel or Egypt or Libya. None of your Cold War stuff."

"Never mind. Let's get down to business. What do we advise Ministers to do about this latest rumour?"

"Not much we can do except make more bloody contingency plans. You've seen the secret Washington telegram..." Feuchtwanger produced it from one of the green files.

Von Sattendorf read through it carefully.

"It's been copied to all our EEC posts and to Moscow. They're bound to react to the report that the other Europeans are to be asked to cut back on their attaché staff as well. By this evening we should have the facts; then I think we recommend that we work out a joint line with the British."

"Not really their business. We have to work unilaterally this time. My own view is—stuff the Yanks. Always has been." Feuchtwanger spoke as if he meant it.

"Put in rather more diplomatic language I hope."

"Not much more. The language of diplomacy is too woolly for these boys. Mainfare and his crowd won't understand unless we talk in monosyllables."

"He's not stupid. He wouldn't be..."

"...where he is if he didn't have something. That's what *Der Spiegel* says this week too. Native cunning, the simple style of the self-made man. A lot of balls."

"He's a powerful Senator."

"Intellect seldom has been a quality overflowing in the American Senate."

"You don't have much time for the country whose relations with us you're meant to look after, do you?"

"Some of the people are all right," Feuchtwanger said grudgingly.

"The ones with German names?"

"Come now. I won't be branded. My remarks started off as referring to the Mainfarers."

"But you don't have much time for any of the present lot do you?"

"Not much. America is supposed to be more mongrel than any other nation under the sun, but their present rulers have more obvious national characteristics than even we Germans."

Von Sattendorf thumbed through one of the files of telegrams in silence. He knew what Feuchtwanger was going to say.

"Naïvety. Others call it directness or honesty."

"Not a very original discovery. Well, after next week it won't be my problem, thank God."

"Oh yes it is original when you rediscover it every day. Any dealings I had with Americans on this desk and I began by thinking it couldn't be true. It usually shows after ten minutes of conversation."

"Let's drop it. You'll be saying they're all Jews next."

"Bad taste, von Sattendorf. Bad taste. You know what I mean." Feuchtwanger looked annoyed for a moment and then shrugged, sat down at the desk facing the other man and they started working on the draft.

Three-quarters of an hour later Feuchtwanger left. They had agreed a line. Von Sattendorf had several pages of scribbled notes in front of him which he would now dictate to Fräulein Helmich. He was proud of his ability to dictate once he had his thoughts marshalled. Secretaries loved it. He never went too fast, never lost the thread, seldom if ever corrected himself. Salem School had been a free educational establishment by German standards, but there had been a classics master there who had taught him technique.

He dialled a three-figure number on his automatic telephone and Fräulein Helmich came in a few urgent moments later in response to his call. Pad and pencil poised, she perched on the edge of the chair right in front of him, chest heaving at the exertion of getting to him quickly enough. Adjusting his notes he was aware without looking up, that her overstretched blouse was still bobbing up and down. It would take a moment or two to settle. This time he moved his eyes slowly up till he reached the round nylon stockinged knees; slightly parted, legs running up unhidden to a barely minimal skirt and a patch of darkness.

"Secret formal Minute, two copies, double spaced," he began. "The Minister will have seen the Secret telegram No. 3914 from Washington concerning the American report of..."

A long morning, half an hour for a canteen lunch, three hours of meetings including one with the Foreign Minister himself, then a further three hours of reports, rewriting telegrams of instructions to London, Paris and Washington. It was five to eight. He was making a few manuscript amendments to one telegram when Fräulein Helmich came in with the final page of his dictation, neat and precise, the way he liked it. He smiled up, tired but pleased. Perhaps it had been too friendly a smile, for she beamed back warmly. Keep it correct, he said to himself. Just to encourage the troops.

"Excellent, Fräulein Helmich. Well done. Sorry to have kept you so late. I hope I haven't spoiled your evening."

"I was going to Cologne but my date had already cried off," she said briefly. "And there's not much to do in swinging Bonn of an evening."

He held his breath. There was a minute's pause as he checked the draft. "Yes, excellent. I think we can pack up now. Thank you and goodnight."

She lingered and helped him clear his trays away. He locked his safe, turned round but she had already disappeared. He put on his coat, took his fur hat from the top of the cupboard, gave a final check to his desk to make sure he had not left any papers out, switched out the light and left the room. As he did so, he realised he had forgotten to buy anything for supper.

Down the conveyor belt elevator, past the guards and out into the night. It was snowing softly; it had been for some time and now it was a couple of centimetres deep.

He had been too busy to notice. The lamplight on the flakes and on the snow-covered ground brought back memories of a childhood; cold memories of a Christmas tree in a British Barrack room where he and some other lucky children from the refugee camps nearby had a fleeting glimpse of warmth and cheer. The rich Christmas food after the cabbage and potato stew in the camp had made him ill. But his two-year-old son now played with the little tin tank he had been given on that occasion. It had worn well for a toy that had once been his only one.

The welcome astrakhan hat down to his ears, coat collar turned up, he made his way out of the Auswärtiges Amt car park and along the road to where his own VW was parked. At the corner of the main road he saw the familiar figure of Fräulein Helmich, gazing (was it with theatrical helplessness?) up and down the street in search of a non-existent taxi. He had to pass her. She turned as he approached. After all the work, he could not but offer her a lift; of course she accepted.

"Where to?"

"Rather out of your way, Herr von Sattendorf," she smiled without much tone of apology in her voice. "Just this side of Mehlem."

"Not more than five minutes. It's a miserable night." Not only her perfume made him aware of her proximity.

They found his car under its layer of snow. It was cold inside but the car started immediately and the efficient heater was soon at work. The drive took fifteen to twenty minutes. A lorry had broken down on a narrow stretch of road and there was a delay at one of the traffic lights. They talked in a desultory, empty way. She said she had a small two-roomed flatlet in an old house. She rented it, on home postings, from an aunt. A bit far out, but she had a car which she used at weekends, and it was cheap.

At the house she inevitably invited him in. He refused, saying he must get back. His wife was away and he had to try and find a late-opening shop to buy something. As soon as he had said it, or perhaps before he said it, he realised he had made a mistake. In certain terms, at least, it was a mistake.

The tiny flat was warmly furnished. A few well chosen pictures and pieces of furniture; a couch, a divan, skin rugs. It was designed for what it was used for and what it was to be used for. Nor did it take long to work round to it. He accepted a whisky and watched while she cooked pork cutlets in the tiny kitchen. She had changed into something that was even more plunging, even more transparent. If it had not been so blatant it would have been crude. She cooked some rice, prepared a winter salad and then threw in an unexpected touch of excellence with a delightfully spiced sweet-sour sauce to cover the meat. The Mosel wine was dry without bitterness.

He relaxed. She already had. He wondered how many of his colleagues had already succumbed. He called her Heidi, she did not call him anything though she knew his Christian name. He wondered what it would be like the next day in the office. Would he be able to work without distraction of guilt? But it was only for another week. The thought was comforting, and it was a further incentive to live dangerously.

She went out to make coffee; he looked casually round the room. On top of a bookcase by one wall there were a number of framed photographs. One was of a woman, so like Heidi that she must be her mother. There were two other photographs, wartime photographs, yellowing with age and lack of fixative. One was of a young man, handsome, fair. He was in the familiar black uniform of the SS. Thousands were. There was another photograph, a group, taken perhaps after some commissioning parade. The fair young man stood out in the middle of the second row. Underneath the photograph the names were printed into the cardboard frame. Wilhelm Schenker, he read.

Heidi came into the room. Von Sattendorf turned towards her, embarrassed at his curiosity.

"Family," she explained. "I don't mind you looking."
"Your mother?"
She nodded.
"Father?"
"Yes."
"Are they..."
"Mother died three years ago at Christmas. As for my father, well ... we lost touch. There was another woman. I use my mother's name."
"I'm sorry."
"No need to be. I don't care much. Sometimes I was curious what happened to him. Mother was sad. He used to send us money from time to time. I think he probably had to keep low after the war for a bit, and it became a habit for him. Not that he did anything wrong. He wasn't at the camps or anything like that. He was in Berlin, at Headquarters."

They changed the subject after that. She sat beside him at the table rather than opposite. Then she put on a record; mood music and a total substitute for speech. She produced some fruit. Her knee touched his and he realised he was being seduced. Another bottle of Mosel was opened, and drunk. Live dangerously. He almost never had since marriage. Uneasily he fumbled a grope at her under the table; unnaturally, a trifle out of practice with strangers. Then they stood up and he was led to the divan.

He woke up at four in the morning after a very brief sleep. He whispered an apology; she nodded, hardly waking. She had heard it before.

CHAPTER EIGHT

Temperly Townsend Jr., State Department, Washington

SOME TIME DURING that same week in late November, Temperly Townsend, Foreign Service Officer, Grade Four, at the State Department took an independent decision and stepped out of line.

Ten minutes late on the day that things came to a head, the school bus pulled away from the front gate, carrying off Melvin, his seven-year-old son. Neither he nor Melvin was particularly happy about attending that particular school, but it was only for another year and then they would be off again abroad, to new educational as well as diplomatic pastures.

Temperly Townsend gulped down the last of his coffee, kissed his four-year-old daughter Kathy, brushed the hairs of the red setter off his trouser leg, shouted an unanswered goodbye to his sleeping wife Claire, and left the house. A three-storey, four-bedroomed house in Albemarle Street in the University Sector, just off Wisconsin Boulevard in the District; a little garden, or rather a patio behind, a two-car garage leading on to the back alley, and he realised how lucky he was that he had bought when he did. Real estate values had shot up. It had cost him around fifty-five thousand, but now it was worth much more. Money made money; his twenty-one thousand a year, about to go up to twenty-four thousand would have gone nowhere if he had had to pay rent. But parental generosity plus a grandfatherly legacy had left him reasonably well-heeled. The Townsend family got by, and had something left over for pleasure, given the odd extra thousand from his wife's inherited dividends.

An onlooker watching Temperly Townsend as he latched the gate behind him and walked down the street to catch his bus might have suspected that here was the all-American civil servant in the traditional mould. And they would have been almost right. Apart from the length of his tousled fair hair which would have raised a frown on his father's face, and the fact that he had not been to church in the last year, he was just that. Features angled enough to stop short of being boyish, tall, athletic build turning rapidly to fat, in all a competent, cheerful, not overbright individual. Reliable and conscientious, his annual reports said. New England son of a Wasp banker; Wesleyan College educated; a history major who had done an early 'sixties version of a year's drop-out in London and Amsterdam and even that had been in the pattern. He had entered the navy at twenty-four, completing three years, first as an ensign from the OCS at Rhode Island, where he had first met Claire. Later he had served on a destroyer in and around Pearl Harbour and rose to the exalted rank of Lieutenant JG. After service he had carried on for a bit in the Reserve, attending meetings and doing the odd summer cruise. But pressures of State Department training and his almost high-society marriage to Claire forced their own priorities and he gave it up. Claire, in her turn the daughter of a Yale professor of economics, was undoubtedly the more accomplished of the two and certainly the least satisfied. She was constantly bored. One reason was that Temperly, while no queer, was one of those peculiarly remote young men that the State Department attracted who were dedicated to their careers and not particularly interested in women.

The State Department opened its formerly glamorous doors to Temperly Townsend and after an initial six months' junior officer training at the FSI just over Key Bridge on the Potomac, he and Claire swept off to the Embassy in London. Both were overjoyed; they were too junior to be over-involved in diplomatic social life and they built up a small tight circle of friends round their South Kensington flat. He was on a rotational programme of on-the-job training in various sections of the Embassy, and he emerged after two years with his own ideas of how diplomacy worked, and with that anglicised transatlantic blend of an accent that is an implicit and criticised part of the make-up of successful State Department officers. London became his emotional home.

Two tours later, one in Accra, the next up the coast in Dakar, had set him in line for being branded an Africanist. He had arrived home, spent the first month of his accrued leave doing up the Albemarle Street house they had bought on their last leave, and then he had gone along to the personnel people to find out about his future. At thirty-five, a Grade FSO 4 with moderately successful reports behind him in the political cone of the service, he was flattered to be appointed on assignment as Special Adviser to the Assistant Secretary for European Affairs. That was about the time Senator Mainfare started being a name to reckon with.

Temperly Townsend caught an L4 bus. His was a one-car family, but it was a Mercedes. His wife needed it but even if she had not, FSO 4s did not get parking facilities at the New State garage. He paid his twenty cent fare and the ride on a good day took twenty minutes: a cent a minute. At the bus queue he had picked up a copy of the *Post* from a news-stand. The front page was covered with pictures and copy about the riots, with foreign news relegated to the end. Not much to cheer up a diplomat there either. The *Post* was making quite sure everyone got full coverage of just how bad a press the States were getting in Europe just now. He knew it from the telegrams, but these days American Embassies were often leaving some things unsaid; posts feared that too much criticism reported might not always find favour in the present climate.

He glanced up from the newspaper: the bus was passing through Georgetown and the street outside the window was crowded with young people, mainly hippies. For a moment he caught sight of a well turned-out man of about his own age, neatly dressed in a dark suit, short-haired, carrying a black briefcase, walking rapidly in and out among the motley of the hippies. How long under Mainfare's influence would it be till they were back to the days when it was a hippy that would stand out? The bus lurched forward and the scene disappeared.

New State Building is between Twenty-one and Twenty-three street. Townsend went round the side and entered by the C street entrance. He showed his security pass to the General Service Guards. There were two of them: an old white man and a younger black. Two or three porters moved across the foyer in front of him, Afro hairstyles bobbing as they shifted a heavy filing cabinet.

He took the elevator to the fourth floor. It had been touch-and-go whether he would move in next to one of the Executive Offices on the seventh, beside his AS, but lack of space relegated him to a larger office, which he had to himself, at the far end of the fourth, facing on to East Street and the protocol entrance. His room had recently been occupied by another General Ops officer working on the southern tier of eastern Europe. A flagged map of Romania was still taped to the wall. Townsend had tried to remove it, but the marks it would have left would be more of an irritant than the appropriateness of its geography to his task.

As he went in to his room Beate shouted to him from her connecting office. The AS was already in. It was the first surprise of the day. Ed Macartney seldom was in before 9.30 but always worked late.

No, blue-rinsed, fifty-year-old Beate Largier did not

know why. Macartney had not asked for Townsend: she thought he would like to know, that was all.

"Quite right," he said. "Thanks."

She had no need of his approbation. Seldom wrong, she was cool, efficient, every inch the California-raised bulldog, with twelve overseas postings to her credit, and personal secretary to Ambassadors for the last four. She was working for Townsend only because of his Special Assistant job. He knew it; she knew it; there was no need to say it; he was always respectfully polite to her. She needed no teaching from him either. She knew how to handle the phone call of a querulous Congressman as well as how to react to the demands of a young FSO 4. But she laughed a lot: they barracked each other: the relationship was good. She took his dictation when he did not type the work himself. She brought his morning coffee in a stainless steel thermos from the cafeteria, placing it on the mat on the desk at the side of the silver-framed photograph of his children.

As Macartney did not contact him, he kept his head down and got on with redrafting the secret Protocol produced by the Department concerning a possible settlement with the European powers over the US bases. The President himself had ordered this after a lengthy session with Senator Mainfare. There was a story that a deal had been struck. In return for support on the internal front, Mainfare had hit out on overseas defence costs. He had called for rapid withdrawal, arguing that it would cost more in the negotiation than letting the billions of dollars of equipment and real estate rot. He had been prevailed upon to avoid making enemies gratuitously, and had eventually made a virtue out of the decision. "Let us save the candle ends then Mr President, but let's do it real fast," he had said. They were to propose a conference in London of all interested parties. And, provided the Europeans agreed, it was to happen soon. The Europeans would protest bitterly at the short notice, but should be given the take-it-or-leave-it message by return of diplomatic telegram.

When the office telephone eventually rang and a voice asked him whether he was free for lunch, Townsend was taken off his guard and mumbled for a few moments before realising it was Ed Macartney himself on the phone.

"Why yes, Sir. Very kind."

"Not kind; working-hard lunch. But we might as well eat well. I'm off to the Hill for the next hour and I'll meet you at the restaurant at one."

Macartney rang off before Townsend could ask which restaurant, and he had to ring the secretary back to ask where she had booked. It was typical of his boss's brisk, brusque but rather absentminded approach. An odd mixture of a man, he was brilliant, or had been. Alert under pressure, when more relaxed he tended to adopt a vague, uncertain and rather nitpicking attitude to his subordinates. He had more or less the same sort of background as his junior except that his father had been Ambassador in London by the end of his career and he was, if anything, more establishment. There was more private money, and he was socially acceptable in Washington society when he wanted to be, which was seldom. This was to the bitter disappointment of his scraggy, vain and bitchy wife who had held him down and back for the previous thirty years. As a hostess, she was not even capable at a dinner table and was totally unable to rise to occasions. She was known throughout the service as 'The Hen'.

Macartney himself had been Minister in London for years and his last overseas post had been as Ambassador to Poland, a job which he had done well through a difficult period. He had impressed some of his visiting superiors, not entirely without cause since his weakness was the greatest of all diplomatic weaknesses, that of saying what you think your audience wants to hear. All things to all men if words alone counted.

After Poland he had scraped a sabbatical year or so as a visiting Professor at the Kennedy School of Government at Harvard. That had been quite a success: he was a good and amusing public speaker and was popular with the students; he latched on to one good idea about European Security in the wake of the disarmament talks and expressed it well on paper. The resultant book, with a lot of gamesmanship underlying it, was a success with a mass rather than an academic audience, some of which latter thought they saw too many borrowed ideas in its pages. Ed Macartney was *made* for the AS job, and so far, with his wife out of the way having her insides removed in a Maryland clinic, he was not doing too badly. And it was now widely speculated that he might be the first career man for years to get the London Embassy as his father had done before him. The job was expected to be available soon.

Townsend was at L'Aperitif Restaurant off Connecticut Avenue at five to one, as befitted a well-trained Foreign Service officer. He found the lunch table, discreetly placed in a corner. He had only been in the restaurant once before. It was way beyond his usual lunch budget with its restrained crystal and cloth, its small tables grouped discreetly with places for only some forty or fifty customers in all. The waiters were French or at a pinch French-Canadian. At the height of anti-de Gaullism they had been jokingly referred to as the Deuxième Bureau. Le Maître recognised everyone: he had that majesty which allowed him to do so, unlike his lesser contemporaries who recognised only the famous. Anyone who came to L'Aperitif was *per se* worthy of note. Temperly Townsend was flattered into having a Bloody Mary while he waited. The Maître got his name and kept using it, which did great things for his morale. At the next table he recognised Senator Hugenot and Cy Hartemann, the Newsweek man, devouring lobster washed with Mateus Rosé. They were giggling together like schoolkids. The words "caught stiff as a ramrod with his pants at half mast" floated across among the chuckles, indicating the high political content of their business lunch.

Ten past one. He was half way through his Bloody Mary and the bowl of crackers. In the corner was a sight that would have made the gossip columnists blow their pen nibs, if Le Maître had let them in. Senator Walters, the recently divorced Junior Senator for Wyoming with the Swedish Ambassador's daughter and the Marvins, Paul and Georgetta, the 'nice young couple', who with their late-late show were hitting the high spots for goodness, light and Christian fellowship these last few Mainfare-orientated months.

The AS appeared, his closely shaven head gleaming in the coyly dull oil lamp light of the restaurant. Ed Macartney walked towards his table, nodded towards Cy Hartemann and an attractive auburn-haired girl sitting with an owl-like White House research staff man with a forehead like a balloon. She smiled her own greeting. The AS had his following.

"Sir. Very nice of you..." Townsend began.

"No charity here boy," was the reply as his chief parked himself opposite. A second Bloody Mary for Temperly Townsend appeared alongside one for Macartney.

"You're doing well, Temp." The beginning was ominous just as the abbreviation of his name was unwelcomely familiar. "I'm doing well too. I like the team we've got. Even Saul of Tarsus, what's his name Saul Tarsana is worth his weight." Saul was the Research Assistant: a good catch and reliable. The AS, Townsend realised with a shock, had been more than drinking. He waited for the punch line.

"You'll both go in the team to the London talks if they get off the ground."

"Great," responded Temperly. That wasn't worth a lunch at L'Aperitif though. He had guessed that Macartney would take them all along. There must be other things in store.

"Of course that's not why we're here spending X to the tenth dollars on lunch."

"Very kind of you, Sir."

"Shut up a moment. Hold the small talk TT, will you." The abbreviation was contrived. He stared hard at his drunk boss. He had never thought ... or was he ill?

"Things is going real bad son. I've just been up on the Hill and one or two of the folk there are real worried. I'm worried too. You let the rot of suspicion set in to our post-war relationships and they'll dissolve into dust in no time. There'll be no pulling back, I tell you."

"I don't think it's as bad..."

"You're young. You don't know. I know. The whole balance of world power is shifting, and it'll shift right off that balance unless something happens. And I won't be part of it."

"There's not much we can do, Sir. The Great American Electorate..."

"You can stuff the electorate. They don't know a bloody thing," Macartney ordered another drink. "I won't be part of it, and that's why we're having lunch together. I'll tell you three things because you're my Assistant and because you've been a good one, and because you ought to be the first to know, and in any case we've never had a meal together. Too bloody mean, my wife always said. Too busy, I say." Macartney smiled a bitter, drunken smile, then poured back the rest of his drink. They ordered fish, and with it some Chablis.

When the waiter had gone out of earshot he went on. "First, you should know that some time ago I was offered the London Embassy. The Ambassador's due to leave soon and I was to be the first non-political appointment there for years."

"Many congratulations, Sir," Townsend burst out.

"Ah, bugger it. Shut up. They've changed their plans and it bloody near kills me. It's what I wanted most in life. I would have accepted the change if it were for a good reason; for a better man, for example, and there are plenty of them around. But that's not the way the game is. They want someone to proscribe ... preside ... what's the word ... over the dissolution of a ... what was it Churchill said?" He paused and forked some fish into his mouth. Townsend did likewise and said nothing. The fish tasted a bit strong, but he spread tartare sauce over the rest of it.

"Yes, they've changed their plans. I'm not to be the straight man at the Queen's Court. They can, and will, and have found someone else to do the work for them. It's part of the cheap package deal that's been done to buy Mainfare's support."

Townsend looked across enquiringly.

"No, not the actor. Mainfare's sidekick: Mr Henry A. Middleton at a guess. It's not sure yet, but that's the way it looks. And it kills me." He poured himself another glass of Chablis, contriving to spill a fair amount on the tablecloth. "Yes, it kills me with jealousy and regret, right in my gut, right here." He made a graphic gesture.

"I'm sorry."

"Sorry, of course you're sorry. Everyone's bloody sorry. The whole bloody world will be sorry." For the first time Macartney raised his voice above the whisper he had been speaking in till then and one or two of the other guests looked across at him with interest.

"And another thing, I've resigned, Temp. I've packed it in. I'm not going to be treated like a..."

Townsend was shocked and looked it. He stared at the older man who was now slouched across the table, the

Chablis glass clutched between his hands as if he were preparing to crush it to splinters between his palms. They sat in silence for a moment or two. Senator Hugenot and Cy Hartemann had stopped joking and were watching from across the room. Perhaps they knew already. Macartney's name had been mentioned enough.

"Ah, the hell, boy. I can't stick it. I'm going. Here's a twenty dollar bill. Fix the check will you when you've finished. I'm sorry to have spoiled our lunch. Maybe later ... maybe later."

"I quite understand, Sir. I'm very sorry," Townsend stuttered out.

"You quite understand? Do you? Well maybe you do. Two decisions like that is a hell too much." Macartney stood up and Townsend followed suit. They shook hands and then Macartney bent over and whispered something in Townsend's ear. "I'm dying Temp. I'm not going to bloody well tell them that, and don't you either. That's not my reason for resigning nor for being screwed sick over the London job. But terminal, inoperable cancer all over my lungs ain't a laughing matter either. No sympathy needed. For some reason there's not much pain, so I'm dying happy." Townsend started to say something, but Macartney silenced him, and then turned and walked stiffly out of the restaurant. Le Maître saw him and went up as if to speak to him, but must have seen the look on his face for he stopped where he was and made a discreet and unacknowledged bow in Macartney's direction. Temperly Townsend finished his fish and most of the Chablis, declined another course but took coffee and camembert, paid the bill and left the restaurant in a strangely remote frame of mind.

It was scarcely two-thirty by the time he got back to the office and already he had a pain in his stomach. He realised that it must have been the fish he had eaten. Beate looked at him oddly as he came in. He wondered if she had heard, but decided it was not up to him to gossip about Macartney's decisions. By three o'clock he was feeling decidedly ill. Then he was sick once or twice and decided to call it a day. He tried to ring his wife, but the phone was engaged, so he got Beate to order him a taxi and went home.

He saw the green Ford Mustang outside his house in Albemarle Street, but was too groggy to pay much attention to it. When he went inside, Claire came down in her dressing-gown looking white and worried. What was the matter, why was he home? Her hair was all over the place, and she had nothing on under her wrap. He went upstairs, Claire fluttering anxiously ahead of him. Why the hell wouldn't she get out of the way? He made a dash for the bathroom just in time. Claire shut the door behind him. As he pressed the flush button he thought he heard a male whisper outside the door. But still it did not register. He heard someone trip on the stairs. It must have been Claire catching the hem of her dressing-gown.

The air in the bathroom must be foul. He moved the catch and tried to open the little window. It would not move at first. He would get round to scraping some paint from the hinges sometime. It had been like that since the bathroom had been decorated in the Fall. Then it opened. He stuck his head out for fresh air and caught a glimpse of a man they had met recently at some party, pulling on his jacket as he darted along the path beside the garage. The man made for the Green Mustang, jumped in and drove off immediately without looking back. He heard Claire creeping back up the stairs. The second and third top steps creaked when one stepped on them. She ought to have remembered that. It was then that Temperly Townsend realised. He drew back from the window and was violently sick once again.

In a way the decision he took was no sudden one. When

the United States Administration loses its grip, half the world could find itself in pieces on the floor. In Temperly Townsend's view the last thirty years had never seen a moment when the world's democracies had been in worse shape. He had long been depressed about the way things were going in American-European relations; his love of Britain and things British did nothing but add strength to his feelings of impotence. He was personally involved; he saw before him the prospect of a broken jigsaw of a once happy picture. The 'Special Relationship' was a stretcher case and for this, while he appreciated that the Europeans might have played the ball-game more fairly and intelligently, he blamed, with a bitter blame, the Mainfarers. Many shared his views, but few in positions in the Administration shared it in such an extreme form. Senate calls for partial troop withdrawals from Europe to show America's Allies that they must foot some more of the bill for their own protection, were one thing. The damage about to be done was in a different league. The damage would be deep; one distrust fed a host of others; it was too late to do anything. Or was it?

Those were some of the reasons which led Temperly Townsend to seek out a man called Rogerson who worked in the information section of the British Embassy in Washington. There were also the deeper reasons. That his boss, Macartney, whom he respected and admired had been turned down for the London Embassy and had resigned the Service; that his wife Claire, whom he did not love but had respected and valued from the point of view of his family life, was being unfaithful to him—though he would not accuse her of it and she would remain in thankful ignorance; that he was still somewhat weak and debilitated from the after effects of a fairly severe dose of food poisoning, were up-to-the-minute reasons for his actions. There were more. He loved Britain and the British. There was no disloyalty there. They spoke the same language, they thought the same thoughts, and they had, or the American white Anglo-Saxon Protestants had, the same ideals and beliefs. One blood; kith and kin; democracies both. No Klaus Fuchs, Rudolf Abel, Burgess, Maclean, Philby, here. There would be no treachery spoken. And one fact passed on about one man, one corrupt man, was nothing about which anyone need call him to hang his head in shame. He might have told the press, the media; he might have done a Daniel Ellsberg, a Pentagon Papers. He would have gained a great audience. But that was not his driving force. Much better to give the information to those who might use it discreetly and well.

Why had he a secret to share? What was the secret? It was not about weapons, not about the US Government's mad policy as he saw it of planning the break-up of the Atlantic links, pulling the carpet out from under its friends and allies. He would have recoiled from any such action no matter how much he disagreed with that policy. But a secret about a man, a man whom the world, if it knew, would condemn, that was different.

The final event that made the worm turn would have affected any man. Ed Macartney left a letter for Temperly Townsend. Townsend was greatly moved that he had been selected. "I hope I do not give you this out of pure bitterness or jealousy," Macartney had written. "But I cannot simply go without some use being made of the information. You, I have got to know only recently. But unlike my long-term friends, you know my recent thoughts." It was a long letter in a large brown sealed envelope. It tended to ramble. There were several documents enclosed, the latest dated the fourth of December, 1967. They purported to tell a story about Henry A. Middleton, the man who was about to play an important role in the affairs of the United States of America. But it was a story, which, if true, gave the lie to the life story as it was generally known, of the future United States Ambassador to London.

Ed Macartney left three other letters; one for his wife; one, a formal one, for the Secretary of State; one for his lawyer. He joked in the last letter about being thoughtful to the end, then he shot himself, cleanly, in the bath.

Townsend took his opportunity two days later at a reception given by a British diplomat at his Maryland home. He had never met Rogerson but he told his host they had an acquaintance in common, and had him pointed out to him. Rogerson was in a corner surrounded by a group of British Embassy people, two or three of them wives. The conversation, as Townsend made his slow way round noisy groups, avoiding waiters with trays crammed with drinks, seemed to be female dominated and to be concerned with the important difficulty of buying good English Stilton in Washington. The woman who was doing most of the talking had a high-pitched, upper-class voice, and the others in the group were beginning to show their dislike of it or her. Rogerson had that particular cocktail party look, pretending to pay close attention to what is being said while at the same time looking around for any non-offensive opportunity to escape. There was a definite skill in cocktail party manoeuvring. Once detached, one then had to avoid routes passing too close to other individuals who might stop and ensnare. Like a game of snakes and ladders, there was a path between the Ancient Mariners, the bores, the too hearty, the silent ones, the whisperers with urgent incomprehensible gossip to impart, those with congenital halitosis and so on. A good diplomat was always armed with a dozen excuses for a move or for not stopping to talk to anyone.' The technique of shaking hands and saying 'Hello, how are you' in half a dozen languages while on the move across a crowded room, in a way that made it clear that that was the extent to which the conversation was to go, was a special art to be learned if giving offence was to be avoided.

Townsend knew many of the faces. He smiled correctly but distantly and came round to face Rogerson. He caught his eye.

"Mr Rogerson?"

"Yes. Hallo. I don't think we've..." Rogerson smiled and pulled himself thankfully away from the group. Townsend backed into a relatively quiet spot and the two men faced each other.

"No, we haven't met. Temperly Townsend. State Department. I am ... was, Ed Macartney's Special Assistant."

"Very sorry about that business." Rogerson turned sombre. Here was something interesting. "He was very ill I hear?"

"Yes," said Townsend briefly. There was a short pause.

"How did you know my name?"

"I knew your name, but couldn't put a face to it." Townsend did not explain. "I also know what you do. You used to attend some of those planning meetings with the CIA and Pentagon Staffs." He kept his voice low.

"Yes?" Rogerson was non-committal, and became a little suspicious.

"I want to talk to you," said Townsend seriously.

"Fine. Go ahead. I don't know why me, but..." Rogerson wondered whether the American had been drinking. He decided that he had not, though he looked strained.

"I'd like to talk in less public surroundings. I have some information which may be of interest to you, to the British Government."

"Hey! What is this, Mr Townsend? Some sort of joke? You playing spies or something? Are you sure you're feeling all right?"

"Yes I'm feeling all right. No I'm not playing spies, nor am I joking. I have some information I wish to pass on through you to your government. Oh, it's not State Secrets, not Pentagon Papers or anything."

"What is it then?"

"It's about a man."

It was touch and go at that point in the conversation whether Rogerson would laugh, back away, make some joke and excuse himself from involvement with a nut-case. But Temperly Townsend was self-evidently not a nut-case. He was an established, middle-ranking American Foreign Service Officer in rather a key position until his boss had shot himself two days previously. So Rogerson hesitated. "But there are established channels of communication between our governments on all matters."

"This is not an American government matter. I am acting as an individual. The information is not a State secret since the State is not aware of it."

"But if they were, it would be State secret?"

"Perhaps."

"Very well. Come to my office tomorrow. Say ten o'clock?"

"Not to the Embassy, and not tomorrow. Tonight."

"Tonight? Is it that urgent?"

"Not so urgent in itself. But urgent in that by tomorrow I may have changed my mind."

"Very well. Will you come to my house? My wife is here. I have to drive her home." Rogerson was unsure how to react. He wanted time to think, talk it over with a colleague, check out Townsend's credentials.

"You have a car outside? Tell your wife you have to go off—you can find an excuse. She can drive herself home. I will be waiting outside in my car in, say a quarter of an hour's time?"

"You've obviously thought it all out. You *are* being serious." Rogerson looked hard at the younger man. "I should really not agree. I don't know you from Adam. You might be anyone..."

"In a quarter of an hour's time. Right outside the gates. I have a white Mercedes 3000."

Rogerson got into the passenger seat. "Where are we going to?" he asked.

"Oh, a bar. Any bar. Away from diplomats. I'm not used to this sort of thing you know Mr Rogerson. I'm no spy. Not that this is treason, treachery. They wouldn't even be able to take me to court if they found out. But they would be annoyed."

Townsend drove for ten minutes; Rogerson lost track of where they were. When they came to a scruffy area somewhere on the outskirts of the city, Townsend pulled up and parked in a side street. They were the only whites around. They went into a bar. It was empty. They ordered drinks and took them to a grimy side-table in a corner. Rogerson for the tenth time that evening wondered if he had a crank with him, wondered why he was there at all, why he was not back with his wife at the cocktail party.

Townsend pulled a bulky envelope out of an inside pocket. "Ed Macartney bequeathed this to me. Here's his letter. I've gone through all the accompanying documents and you'll find they make compulsive reading. Bar one or two gaps it's a pretty invincible case. I have kept no copies, no written record, no evidence that I ever had or saw these documents. If you use them well, they may do some good. I hope so. I hope so."

Rogerson was not a brilliant man, nor was he aware of all the high-level political gossip. But he was methodical, painstaking, optimistic. He read through the documents then and there. By the end, his worst suspicions had been confirmed and he had wasted an evening. He made to hand them back. "Good material for a novel," he said slowly. "Nothing more. Here, have them back. There's nothing in it for us." They had both long finished their drinks, but neither had ordered another. The Negro bartender was watching an old movie on the television and was in no hurry to press them.

Townsend did not look discouraged. He had been expecting it. He was not brilliant either, but he was dedicated and had thought things out. "No, I won't take them back and I was aware you might react this way. I would have done the same. You have a reputation for being cautious; did you know? But I'll take them back tomorrow if by then you want to part with them. In the meantime, show them to your Political Counsellor, Mr Halley, Peter Halley. Ask him what he thinks. Will you do that?"

It was getting late. Rogerson was thinking of his wife's irritation when he had shot off leaving her to drive herself home. He should get back and start placating her. Enough was enough and Townsend was definitely under some strain. He'd have a word with someone in the morning.

"OK," he said, "come and collect them any time after lunch." Rogerson smiled. "I'll get Peter Halley to look at them, of course, but if you think there's anything in all this er ... material for us, I think you'd better think again. My suggestion is that you get a good night's sleep. That's what I would do. You've obviously had a ... what I mean is that with Mr Macartney's death..."

"Oh, I know what you mean, Mr Rogerson. But do me a favour and just show the stuff to Halley in the morning. I'll ring you at lunchtime and see if you still want me to collect. I'll come at once if you do; if you want to keep the stuff, that will be my part in the matter at an end and you won't be troubled again." Townsend paused. "Now, I'll give you a lift home."

"Oh, that won't be necessary," said Rogerson hurriedly. "I'll get a cab. I'm not more than a quarter of an hour away..."

Peter Halley was busy. He had a number of letters he

wanted to get into that day's diplomatic bag to London. He was abrupt with Rogerson, a man he found slow and dull and for whom, in consequence, he had little time. Rogerson said he felt duty-bound and so on. He was sorry to disturb. He left the bulky envelope lying on Peter Halley's desk.

It was eleven o'clock before Halley looked at the contents. Mad letters came in by every post, but this was an odd source. He thought he remembered Temperly Townsend. A tall blond all-American straight up and down man. Hardly a crank. He started reading. Half way through the second document he came across Middleton's name and let out a low whistle. Then he pressed the buzzer for his PA. 'Dorothy, see if H.E.'s free. In about half an hour would be best. Yes, in half an hour. And get them to keep the bag open till the last moment."

Temperly Townsend rang at four. Rogerson was in a bit of a panic. Yes, they'd like to keep the papers. Could he come round and discuss it with Peter Halley? But no, Temperly Townsend had slept a night on his deed, and was sticking rather fearfully to his part of the bargain. As far as he was concerned there was no envelope and he had never seen any papers or anything.

Some two weeks later Temperly Townsend received a posting order—to New Delhi. His wife Claire decided that she was staying in Washington. The children could come out to India for holidays from time to time. It suited them both.

CHAPTER NINE

Foreign and Commonwealth Office, London, S.W.1

Pringle went to stay with some friends near Tenterden in Kent and came back on the afternoon of Sunday the twenty-fifth of November. Because of the heavy weekend traffic, he drove at a snail's pace through south-east London. He was back in his flat by about six, listened to the news and took a whisky to his bath. Then he got casually dressed and went to spend the evening with the Duty Resident Clerk, Richard Thain. He was a friend who had joined the Service at the same time as Pringle and with whom he had shared a flat for a blissful, if rather drunken, five months before he had decided to go through with his marriage to Helen. Thain had come to the wedding and, staying more sober than most of the other guests, had left with an opinion of Pringle's wife that he was only to share five years and one divorce later, or so he kept telling him. They now agreed about her.

He was a bachelor, this stipulated by the Office as being necessary for a Resident Clerk, living in reasonable comfort and lack of expense in a not unattractive small suite of rooms in the top north-west corner of the Office, overlooking both St James's Park and Horse Guards. It was worth the one or two sleepless nights a week on duty and the problems and frustrations of constantly living on top of one's job. He liked it. Pringle regretted never having had the opportunity, the odd flirtations with power that were offered by looking after Britain's international posture at night while all else except the messengers, the cipher clerks and the communications people who kept the Office alive out of hours, were asleep or at leisure. While the Embassy in Saigon or Tokyo or Washington worked, time-lag or no time-lag, London had to be superficially awake as well. The Ambassador in Vientiane was on the phone one moment; a telegram from Seoul needed a reply the next; but there were also other parts of Whitehall, the House itself, Ministers at home after good dinners, all needing late night attention. Pringle remembered the story of Thain's first telephone call when he had come on duty for the first time. His predecessor, moving out to live with an out-of-work actress in Swiss Cottage had explained the ropes rather too swiftly, told him that nothing was happening, that it never did on a Saturday night after ten in the evening. Then he left. The telephone had rung immediately and a voice at the other end had said "Resident Clerk? Duty Officer Number Ten here. The Prime Minister wants a word with you." Click, click, then a pause and Thain had had to stumble through his interpretation of what was currently going on between India and Pakistan to the Prime Minister who had explained that he had with him an important and self-important dinner guest who was lecturing him, and he needed something with which to hit back. It had been sufficient and the PM had written a note on the Monday to the Secretary of State congratulating him on the quality of his night staff. It would help Thain's career prospects, though that was now three Prime Ministers ago. They had lived through a few.

This night began quietly. Thain had invited his current girl friend up to keep him occupied if Pringle failed, and to cook them both dinner in the Clerkery kitchen. She produced an unexciting chicken casserole, partially pre-cooked, but there was a large bottle of chianti from Del Monico's in Soho which, because Thain was not drinking much being on duty and because she had only a glass, helped Pringle's evening along well.

About ten, the phone started ringing a lot; a consular case of a tourist killed in a car crash in Vienna, and the business of getting on to the local police in the man's home town to break the news to his wife and next of kin. There was a batch of telegrams from Washington about the latest moves there, which Pringle knew could wait till the morning. There was a blurred phone call from a junior Minister in the Department of the Environment who had obviously been dining well, complaining that the Foreign Office was not doing enough for some constituent of his in prison in Turkey for drug smuggling. Thain gave a superb performance of diplomatic conciliation and explanation to the Minister who hung up, duly consoled by the belief that his problem would be put to the Foreign Secretary and absolutely everyone else concerned with the minimum possible delay.

While Thain was on the phone to Welfare Section about the disappearance of a Counsellor in some remote African post, one of the three other phones rang and Pringle fielded it for him. It was the Foreign Secretary's Principal Private Secretary, one of his four diplomatic grade personal assistants. Pringle explained, or began to explain who he was, that he wasn't on duty. He knew the PS slightly, a cold, efficient man with little humour and no friends whom he had ever heard declare for him. The PS was not interested. Pringle was there, he was a member of the Office; there was something to be done. Pringle started to explain again.

"Just take a bloody message, will you," said the less than polite voice at the other end. Pringle apologised, switched on the scrambler phone and started writing.

The Foreign Secretary had also been weekending out of town, with the ebullient Commander Whitney MP at his home near Brighton. Saturday evening there had been a mixed bag at the dinner given in his honour. Dr Pickforth of Sussex University had been one of the guests. He was scarcely the Foreign Secretary's ideal dinner companion, but he was Vice-Chairman of Whitney's Constituency Association and they sat next to each other.

Commander Whitney was proud of having an academic of Pickforth's standing in his Association: it added tone and intellect to the selection of retired military personnel and minor landed-gentry who otherwise filled the committee. He briefed the Foreign Secretary firmly on this in advance, and Whitney was one of the most important of the back-benchers. Reluctantly, therefore, the Foreign Secretary listened when Pickforth told his story about a war diary which he had come across, written on parachute silk. He seemed to think it was important evidence of an escape by high-ranking Nazis at the end of the war. To historians it might be exciting, but the Foreign Secretary had more topical problems on his mind. He left the dinner early, very bored and not at all impressed by his table companion nor by what he judged to be a very far-fetched story indeed. He almost said so, but then he saw Whitney watching him across the port, and instead smiled reassuringly as he had done with cranks all his life, and said he would get the Office to follow it up and let Pickforth know.

Sitting back thankfully in the rear seat of his official Humber he made a note on the back of an envelope to ring his Private Secretary about it. At the same time he made a mental note to avoid functions run by Whitney in future. Now he knew why the man had never held any ministerial office. And what a choice of dinner companions; the standard of some dons at these new universities was deplorable.

The next morning, Pringle went along to the Germany Desk Officer to offload the Secretary of State's war diary story on to him. He was puzzled, but said he would follow it up. Pringle told him what little he knew about Pickforth, explaining a fraction bitterly that he seemed to be doing most of the Germany Desk work as well with all the Library files he had been landed with. The other man commiserated a trifle insincerely. "You chaps with your splendid language proficiencies," he smirked.

Pringle went back to the files. There was still a lot to read; then he would have to write the report.

The telephone rang about half an hour later. It was the Germany Desk Officer. "Sorry, man. I should have been happy to browse through Pickles, sorry, Pickforth's war diary, but I've been overruled. You're our current liaison man with history it seems, and the powers-that-be want both the Pickforth requests to be kept under the one thumb. It's all yours. Dreadfully sorry, and all that." He rang off.

What powers-that-be? Pringle's work for American Department was suffering enough as it was, and Anderly was getting restless. The priorities were getting muddled, and so he decided to tell Anderly the latest score. Anderly was indignant. "You're in American Department, not in War Records Research." As Pringle left him, he was ringing everyone up including the Principal Private Secretary. About ten minutes later he came into Pringle's office with a long face.

"Everything stops for a PQ," he said. "It's all yours."

"Is there a Parliamentary Question down?" Pringle asked. "I understood from Library that Pickforth would wait a bit longer before stirring things up."

"Private Office say that you started on this thing. You are the expert. You finish it and then you can get on with your departmental work. That's that." He sounded as if he thought it was Pringle's fault. "And a lot of use it is having you in the department in the present crisis when you have to spend an age digging around with centuries-old files. What Research Department and the Historical Advisers are doing I don't know. I tried to pass it on but

I've been sat upon." He put on a convincing show of being very angry.

"Trouble is I speak German and Serbo-Croat."

"Bloody mad. We've got a crisis on and you're shipped off to the past..." He raged on for a minute or two more and then slammed out of the room, reappearing two minutes later. "Oh, I forgot. You've to go up and see Security. They've heard what you're doing."

"Why on earth? What's Security to do with these papers?"

"Don't ask me. Ask Miller. He's expecting you to ring."

Pringle rang Miller a few moments later. He said not to bother coming round. He was abrupt about it. They could talk in the car next day. They were going down to Brighton to see Dr Pickforth. Would Pringle fix it up directly with Pickforth, making sure he would be available? Miller had an official car on call. Say a meeting at eleven-thirty? It would mean a fairly early start.

Pringle duly tried to ring Pickforth. It took ages to get through and when he did Pickforth did not sound very impressed at the idea, but agreed in the end. He never asked why they were coming and Pringle did not feel it necessary to explain.

The car, with Miller already in the back, called at eight-thirty. It was a light green Ford not from the usual car pool. The chauffeur was wearing tweeds and had a brown felt hat stuck on the back of his head. It struck Pringle that driving wasn't his main profession. He could have been a retired policeman.

Miller began discussing the previous Saturday's Calcutta Cup game. But behind the chat he was serious, not just in the aftermath of England's defeat at Murrayfield.

"We have to get Pickforth to lay off," he said earnestly, then followed it up with a quick grin. "We descend on this don together and tell him we shove him into Brighton clink unless he belts up."

"Sorry?" Pringle said, bewildered. "I thought all he was doing was following up some historical lead to do with post-war remnants of Nazism."

"Bit more than that."

"What, then?"

"We've been following it in a desultory way for some time. Clearing house for all these rumours of Martin Bormann living it up in some South American jungle etcetera etcetera. Publicity gambits and cranks for the most part. But then one or two irrefutable facts came to light. People with Third Reich histories in strange places doing strange things. Pickforth picked up something at a recent conference in Tel Aviv. That is why he's making the fuss."

Dr Thomas Pickforth was a taut red-haired man with a nose that jutted out of his face at the wrong angle. His high cheekbones were flushed as if he were perpetually on the point of being very angry indeed. His head was joined to his body by a neck which was equally wrongly angled, giving his whole bearing an aggressively uncomfortable look, and the impression was finished off with a chin that was up in the air as if he were tempting anyone to punch it.

The chin was first round the door and into the room where his visitors were waiting for him. Pickforth smiled thinly at them, took them to his study and immediately offered tea.

"That's what you people always drink," he said. If it were meant as a joke, it came across as a simple statement of fact.

They sat around on shabby modern chairs, which had been badly designed and, though they could not be more than two years old, they were already faded and torn. Pickforth picked up a phone and persuaded someone who was evidently far from willing to bring in tea. It arrived ten minutes later, lukewarm and weak, slopped down in front of them by a skinny, bitter-looking secretary. Until it arrived they talked generalities, the frustrations of working at a new University, the latest student revolt, the cost of housing in the South East.

As soon as the woman had slammed her way out of his study, Pickforth said: "Well that's quick work; a bloody sight quicker than Janet and her tea. I spoke to your boss on Saturday night. I was expecting a brush-off letter in a week or two's time. Either you diplomats haven't enough to do, you're scared stiff of the Foreign Secretary, which I doubt, or I've hit on something important after all. I always had a suspicion you lads were hiding something behind your backs." His awkward nose waved up and down in the air as he spoke. There was a tinge of dislike in his voice, born of an unease which Pringle had come across among many academics when dealing with civil servants—the theorisers believing they knew more than the doers, yet envying their ability to act instead of preach. There were jealousies in the other direction too.

"Nothing like that at all," said Miller breezily. "We've been asked to come down and see you simply to have a look at the document, if you don't mind."

"Which document? The diary or the other papers? If it's the latter, I haven't got them yet. Your library is still sitting on most of them."

"Sorry, my fault," Pringle broke in. "I've been a bit pressed..." Miller looked at him with some irritation; it wasn't the moment to start explaining to Pickforth how things were.

"A bit pressed, eh? These papers are nigh on thirty years old, laddie and you're not old enough to have been sitting on them that long. What are you hiding? That's what I want to know. And I want to know quick. I've got this manuscript at the publishers' right now, and they're holding it up for me in the expectation of a last good chapter. I want that book out soon. Publish or be damned; that's university life. I've got my future to think of and this is my big work. I want the stuff now," he repeated.

"The diary?" asked Miller. "Could we perhaps have a look at it?"

"You scratch my back, Mr Miller. Yes, you can see it. I don't think it's very important, you know, but quite interesting nonetheless. You heard how I got hold of it?"

"A little."

Pickforth started to tell them about the Major's find. "Bought the suit at a jumble sale; would you believe it? They are a toffy-nosed pair, the Major and his wife, but all right at heart. They made me promise not to tell anyone so I'd be glad if you keep that bit to yourself." He opened a battered filing cabinet and took out a brown envelope. He shook the contents gently out on to the desk.

"It's in fairly good nick. The silk is sound but some of the ink has faded and run badly, particularly on the outside. Must have got pretty wet at some stage, or it may have been dry-cleaned."

They bent over and looked at it together. Miller eventually said, "Could we take it away, photograph it and get it deciphered by experts? We'll be most careful with it."

Pickforth paused a moment, looked thoughtful, stared at the diary and then back at them. Then he said slowly: "Answer, no. I don't think I trust you. I would in other circumstances, but not right now. I'm not a complete twit Mr Miller. I think I may have something here, otherwise ... It is not just the historical interest that sent down to me two obviously high-powered FO men at a moment's notice. It's got to be a lot more than that. Could it be, could it be as I said to the Foreign Secretary, something to do with what I heard in Tel Aviv the other week? Could it Mr Miller? And then these files that have mysteriously turned up, found at the back of some old cupboard, so you tell me. I found it a bit strange when I was told about that at first. The Public Records Office released the other files with lots of cross-references, so I knew they must exist. Then why were they not released at the same time? I have always felt that the good old FO wasn't the most efficient of our government organisations but you're not that inefficient. Little things are beginning to hang together now, and it's just not good enough. You can go back and tell your bosses that. Now, if you don't mind, **I have a lecture** straight after lunch and I have some preparation to do for it." He stood up, his chin swaying angrily. The phone on his desk rang and he went across to answer it. He stood with his back towards them, mumbling into the mouthpiece, gazing out of the window at a group of students who were making their way along a path to one of the new lecture halls.

"Guessed as much," Miller whispered. "Could have bet that's how he would react. But, we've done some research on him. We can't really force him. It would cause too much of a stink, but I think I have the right bait. Just wait for some of Miller's Ambassadorial-style diplomacy coming up." He giggled silently. Pringle stared back uncomprehendingly.

A few moments later, Pickforth finished his phone call and turned back to them. He was polite but distant. "Sorry about that," he said. "Now I really must go." He gathered up the silk diary and carefully re-inserted it in the brown envelope.

"Just one more minute of your time, Dr Pickforth," Miller said seriously. "As you have realised, there is more in this than is immediately obvious."

"As I thought." Pickforth sat down again and stared at them.

"And I have, in consequence, been sent down with my colleague here to see you and to ask you, on behalf of the Secretary of State, if you would consider joining us on a sort of Select Committee of Enquiry. The Secretary of State personally would value it greatly if you felt you could spare the time."

"What sort of Select Committee?" Pickforth looked more interested.

"A non-public one."

Pickforth's face fell. "I am afraid..." he began.

"I have been asked to appeal to you to join us as 'the expert'. It will be a very high-powered committee. You may not be aware, but a great deal is, or could be, at stake."

"My book is at stake. There's the chance of a Chair..."

"The security of the State ... But I need not preach to you Dr Pickforth. I know that you will appreciate, when you hear the details, why you, with your expertise, are needed. We have a great deal of information, delicate, secret information. You would have to sign the Official Secrets Act of course."

"I've done that before, when I did Military Service."

Miller's hooked him, Pringle thought. He was still confused.

'It could lead to other government-sponsored work Dr Pickforth. Most important to get in on the inside. You would be paid, and I have been authorised to say that you would be permitted special access to papers which are still subject to the Act. You would of course be allowed to publish at the end, everything that is publishable that is."

"In thirty years' time of course," Pickforth tried to sound severe.

"We have instructions to act at once. Events dictate a report to Cabinet by this time next week. Select Committees don't always take years."

"I can't get away."

"Secretary to the Cabinet can ring your Vice-Chancellor before lunch. It's all laid on. We'll wait and take you up with us in the car. We have a room booked for you at the

St Ermins Hotel so that you are nearby. You're a bachelor aren't you?"

"So?"

"All the less arrangements to make."

"I'll have to tell the Dean."

"Leave that to the Vice-Chancellor. May I use your phone?"

"Of course. I'll go and pack." Pickforth's chin had taken on a less aggressive angle. Even the nose looked more subdued, but his cheekbones were more flushed than ever. He left the room rapidly.

"If you can't beat them get them to join you," Miller said with a cynical smirk. "It will keep him quiet and we'll have the diary. It's a shade more moral than pinching it, which was the other alternative."

"What was that bit about him having picked up something in Tel Aviv? The Private Secretary didn't mention that bit of information."

"I don't know the whole story, but he heard something about an escape from the Führerbunker in April 1945. They got out via Spain, and there was a lot of money involved, including some which came from a source in London. We'll get the full story from him later. Meanwhile, we'd better start our own enquiries into where this diary came from."

CHAPTER TEN

Major Wilfred Turton, J.P., R.A. (Retd.), Kent

MAJOR TURTON WAS in his garden again on Thursday the twenty-ninth of November. It was eleven in the morning, a cold early winter one, and he was about to go indoors for his morning coffee. The visitor came round the side of the house, coughed discreetly and waited till the Major got up from his knees, where he had been planting-out cabbage seedlings.

"Major Turton? Sorry to bother you. Didn't ring the doorbell, looked over the fence and thought it would be you."

The Major gave a friendly smile. "Can I help you? Sorry I don't think we've met. Unless, wait a bit. You were in the Gunners too. May, no later, July, 1944, Sicily. Captain ... Captain. Never forget a face."

The visitor looked taken aback. He had come with a purpose. This was out of schedule. But then, "Yes," he said, "come to think of it, I do think your face is..."

"Come inside, come inside. This needs a drink. Your name, I'm sorry, I have a dreadful memory for names." The Major spoke as if they had last met the previous day.

"Browne. Browne with an 'e'."

"Ah yes. Captain Browne. Was it Dick?"

"Henry."

"What will you have Henry?"

They settled down with a drink. The Major could hear his wife moving about upstairs. He hoped she would not come down in her curlers. He'd go up and warn her. "Clever of you to have spotted me over the fence like that," he said.

"'fraid it wasn't quite like that, Major."

"Call me Wilfred."

"Yes, Wilfred. Come down to see you, actually old man. Didn't realise..."

"How very nice. Regimental Association? 'fraid I never really bothered to keep in touch."

"No, no. That is ... er ... it's about your discovery."

"Discovery? Discovery? Sorry, don't get it. Sure you haven't got the wrong man? But first things first, Dick."

"Henry."

"Yes. Sorry, Henry, of course. Whisky?"

"Gin and T if you have it."

"Sure thing. Ice?"

"No thanks. Spoils a good drink."

"Quite so. Now what was it ... er ... er ... Henry?" The Major settled back comfortably in a chintz-covered chair. There was a bang from upstairs. "Just the wife," he said. "Spot of the old housework."

"This diary on parachute silk."

"Oh yes?" Major Turton looked across at his visitor. "How did you hear about that?" April seemed a long time ago.

"Dr ... Dr ... Pickforth was it?"

"He was on to you was he? I say, you're not from the National War Museum or something?"

"No, no."

"Nice chap, Tommy."

"Who?"

"Tommy Pickering. Where did you meet him, er ... Henry?" He had forgotten about the diary. Tommy had never given it back.

"Strictly speaking, I haven't. You see I'm working for the Ministry of Defence, now. Civilian job of course."

"But you must ... well, you must be creeping up to retirement, if you don't mind me saying so."

"Quite right. Sixty-seven actually. But I've got one of

these jobs ... well, never mind. I came to see you about the diary. You see my office heard about the diary and now has actually seen it. Now we are trying to trace its history."

"Working backward, eh?"

"Working backwards."

"Tommy not tell you?"

"Dr Pickforth said that it would be better if we asked you direct."

"Quite right too. Wife would have got a bit upset if he had said. As for myself, it doesn't matter to me. Quite funny really and it's a very good suit after all."

Two in the afternoon after a light omelette lunch, Major and Mrs Turton and Mr Browne—he insisted that he had dispensed with his military title—went together in an official car to look for a church in a scruffy part of south-east London. It took them an hour to get to the outskirts and another hour and a half to identify the church. It had happened quite a while ago. In the event, and with the prospect of something out of the ordinary to occupy the afternoon, Mrs Turton had swallowed the embarrassment and co-operated to the full. Something Mr Browne had said had reassured her that his investigations would not lead to the neighbours discovering that she had once bought a second-hand suit in a church jumble sale. Beside her on the back seat the suit itself lay wrapped in brown paper. It was going back to the Ministry with Mr Browne for investigation.

The church, with wire mesh over the windows and barbed wire around the cornices to deter vandals, was locked. The billboard outside was defaced and the address of the vicar was unreadable. The organist's address was just legible, but when they got to his house there was no reply. Eventually the local police station was resorted to. Mr Browne produced an identity card and got immediate assistance. The Station Sergeant himself came with them in the car to show them the vicarage.

The vicar was in. So were at least ten of his, or someone else's, children and it was difficult to conduct a formal enquiry. But in the event it was easier than everyone had expected. The vicar remembered the occasion of the fête, Mrs Turton's brief visit, and, surprisingly, that particular suit.

"Why do you remember it so clearly?" asked Mr Browne cautiously. He had to repeat himself above the noise of fighting, screaming children.

"I thought of buying it myself. I might have done at the end of the fête if it had been left unsold. On the other hand..." the vicar paused uncertainly.

"On the other hand what, Vicar?" asked Mr Browne raising his voice above the hubbub.

"Well, I ... I knew where it came from. I'm most frightfully sorry, but normally when one buys second-hand goods one is unaware of their history. I might have felt a bit..."

The others waited patiently while the vicar disentangled a screaming small child's hair from the hinge of a wooden climbing frame.

"Yes?" said Mr Browne after the rescue operation was complete.

"I'm not quite sure about my facts. I think you'd be better asking the police. They've probably got a record. I should think we got it from them about the end of October, 1972. No. It would be a bit earlier than that, about the end of August, because we had it cleaned thoroughly. It needed it and there was nothing to be gained by taking risks, even though the police said it had been fumigated."

"Oh my goodness," said Mrs Ethel Turton, half to herself, half aloud. The vicar was quite sure about his facts but delicacy forebade him to explain what they were.

The Station Sergeant from the first police station directed them to the second station at Tower Hamlets. When the Sergeant had left, Mr Browne explained that he wasn't really meant to use the police, but it did save so much time.

At Tower Hamlets, the Station Sergeant there, having been shown Mr Browne's identity card, looked up his log book and daily incident registers. He checked through a list of old vouchers, then eventually, lacking any briefing about the present ownership of the suit, bluntly told them where it had come from. A pair of silver cuff-links had been similarly disposed of. There had been nothing to identify the dead man found beside the quay and Mr Browne seemed disappointed. The coroner's report and the initial police reports provided a little background which might give the Ministry some further leads.

Major and Mrs Turton got home about eight-thirty that night. They did not talk very much during the journey. "No," they had said to Mr Browne. No, they did not want the suit back after all. The Ministry could keep it or dispose of it as they wished.

Foreign and Commonwealth Office, London, S.W.1

Miller went along with Pringle on the Friday to see Gilbert Winter. He had asked for a resumé of the evidence in the light of Browne's report. Pringle began with the parachute-silk diary. "Through a chain of circumstances which I won't bother you with," he said, "this was found sewn into the sleeve of a suit which we managed to trace back to a man of about seventy to eighty years of age. To be more precise is difficult, for his body was found at the end of August, 1972, beside a wharf at the West India Docks. The police evidence subsequently presented to the Tower Hamlets Coroner was, according to all the records, fairly skimpy, but there was nothing to suggest foul play. It was estimated that he had fallen; they identified where his head had struck the ground. One police officer who remembered the case said he was impressed by the good condition of the man's clothing and boots, and by a pair of unidentified silver cuff-links, which have not been traced, since they were sold by the police to defray funeral expenses. An estimated three weeks had passed before the man's body was found, setting the date of death on or about tenth August. We have not requested a post-mortem since, in the circumstances and with the length of time that has elapsed, we are assured by expert opinion that this would be unlikely to reveal much. No identification marks were noted on the body, though the Coroner himself speculated that the man might either be foreign or a sailor, since his skin was highly tanned.

"The diary itself, if such a slim document could be called a diary, passed into the hands of Dr Pickforth, who is a Lecturer in Modern European History at Sussex. With his subsequent co-operation, we have subjected it to an initial series of photographic and X-ray enlargements and have been able to decipher the vast majority of the document. The beginning is written in ordinary German, the latter parts are in a type of shorthand commonly used in Germany during the War. It records a journey made by the writer, with some others. It began in the Führer-bunker early on Sunday, twenty-ninth April, 1945 and ended on an estate in the jungles of Paraguay some months later. It is written in abbreviated form, often giving little else than time and place, though the tensions and trials undergone by the members of the party, the constant anxiety about being discovered, and the depressions resulting from the news that reached them about the state of defeated Germany, show through clearly from time to time. The central figure in the journey is not the writer of the diary, and is known simply as the Commander, some high Nazi, possibly even Martin Bormann himself. The route of their escape is recorded; there is a rough map drawn of the journey from Berlin to Spain. The other members of the group are either called by their Christian names or given a code number. Only one, a man called Wilhelm Schenker is named in full. The only reason for this appears to be that the writer of the diary did not like or trust this man Schenker. We have identified him from the diary, and from the Library files, as having been a junior *Aide de camp* to Hitler himself. There is little else in the diary as such, but it does provide *prima facie* evidence of an escape, as yet undocumented, of a prominent Nazi or Nazis from Berlin on the day that Hitler committed suicide. The supposition is that the old man in whose suit the diary was found was the diarist; the indications from the text are that he was the most junior member of the party, possibly a steward or valet to the man known as the Commander. He may have kept it for sentimental reasons, or conceivably as an insurance policy."

"Blackmail?" Gilbert Winter broke in then.

"Could be," Pringle said. "But the death was pretty certainly accidental if that's what you're thinking."

"Pickforth found this document particularly interesting," he went on, "firstly because he had come across it before any other historian and it was his own possession so to speak. Secondly, it documented an unrecorded escape from the ruins of the Third Reich, and thirdly, because, on the last page, it named two or three people outside defeated Germany, who appear to have helped this group in one way or another, by providing refuge, a plane on one occasion, and a very substantial sum of money on another. A famous Spanish count, now dead, who had strong pro-Nazi leanings, provided a staging post of refuge at his house to the south of Madrid. An expatriate German university lecturer in Madrid bought the plane for the journey to South America, since the German military machine which had taken them thus far would have been too recognisable. Someone in London with the name Benner is recorded as having sent 'the funds in his keeping' to finance the journey, and a man in the States, known simply as the 'American Leader', also sent money from 'emergency funds in his keeping' to the group's South American destination. A further German expatriate owned the unidentified jungle estate where the party ended up."

"Interesting as all this is," Pringle went on, "there seems little of relevance to us now, even though it may be fascinating to Dr Pickforth and his fellow historians—that is, assuming the diary itself is not an elaborate forgery. On this point expert opinion is convinced that the type of silk and indelible ink used fits in with the claimed date and country of origin. The purpose the writer had in keeping the diary remains obscure, but he may have felt he was recording something which might, some day, be of historical importance, or, as I said earlier, as an insurance policy.

"Benner, the Englishman with the unusual name, we have identified from the files as Geoffrey Benner, now Sir Geoffrey Benner, MP, on whom we have a wealth of information which points only too clearly to where his wartime sympathies lay.

"A further small straw which has added life to this particular train of enquiry is provided by Pickforth who told us, in his new capacity as member of the Select Committee, that while attending a recent conference of academics in Tel Aviv, he discussed his pet subject of Neo-Nazism with a colleague, a man who had been a former British civil servant and is now an Israeli citizen.

This man told Pickforth that he remembered seeing evidence, dated as late as 1950 or 1951, that a major escape of senior Nazis had been effected from Berlin on the night of the twenty-eighth to twenty-ninth of April 1945, with the help of German Government money which had been secretly held in London throughout the war, as a contingency against such an eventuality. This ties in circumstantially with the mention of Benner in the diary, and this story, coupled with evidence in the diary, was the one which Pickforth pieced together and regaled to the Secretary of State at the dinner party last week.

"But having looked at it all fairly carefully, I must say that unless we see something to be gained by raking this muck up and discrediting Sir Geoffrey Benner who, as far as we know, has led a fairly blameless life in recent years, we should put a submission to the Secretary of State, get him to thank Pickforth warmly for his help, give the public the files, with the exception of the stuff on Benner which would cause a political fuss, and then proceed to forget about the whole thing."

Gilbert Winter agreed, and that was the way they left it, until they heard from Peter Halley.

CHAPTER ELEVEN

Foreign and Commonwealth Office, London, S.W.1

Pringle had heard nothing at all from the girl Helen since she abandoned him outside the Vauxhall restaurant some weeks before. He knew she had rung once, but he had no way of contacting her and his attempts to find out where she came from or where she lived via his Stockwell party-giving acquaintance led nowhere. He didn't know the girl either, and he couldn't identify the man she had been with when she first came to the party. It was sad, but Pringle was busy and had one or two girl friends who were generally available any time he felt the urge for a brief cohabitation.

She rang him in the office that same Friday. He was busy on another of his phones and his secretary fielded the call for him.

"I asked if you could ring her back," she said. "But she insisted on waiting."

"Hello?" Pringle said. "Sorry to keep you waiting."

"Hello. It's Helen."

He immediately thought for some absurd reason that it was his wife who had contrived to disguise her upper-class whiney voice.

"Pause, two, three..." said the voice at the other end of the phone.

"Oh, Helen," he said. "How nice. I tried to get in touch..."

"How nice," she mimicked. "How nice to be remembered. How are you?"

"Well, thanks." He remembered her technique. He had to attack first. "How about dinner tonight?" he said abruptly. "Pick you up at seven-thirty, OK?" It was a challenge. He was sure she wouldn't accept and in any case he had something else on.

"Fine," she said. "Can you pick me up here?"

"Oh ... er ... yes. Where's *here*?"

"You don't sound very happy that I've agreed to meet you."

"I am. I am, really, I am. Just a bit rushed, that's all. Give me your address. I've got a pencil."

She read it out. Classy one, but he didn't think more about it till seven that evening. In the meantime he had lost another friend by crying off his dinner engagement.

A policeman on the pavement checked Pringle's credentials. He had to show him his driving licence and an office pass before he was allowed near the German Ambassador's Residence. He rang the bell. A steward in a white jacket answered immediately. It was then he remembered that he didn't know her surname.

"Yes. Please?" The steward had a German accent.

"Miss Helen..."

"Ah, Miss Kuhl. Is she expecting you, Sir?"

"Er, er ... yes," Pringle said, wondering if it could be some elaborate joke. The German Ambassador's namesake —at a guess a daughter.

Helen appeared in the hallway, smiling. "Hi," she said. "Just on time. Very punctual. My father would approve."

"You're not the genuine thing? Not H.E.'s daughter are you?"

"Afraid so. Didn't I say? Perhaps I didn't. You're not overawed, are you?"

"Er, couldn't say that exactly. Just startled. Bit much for a mere First Secretary."

"Ah," she said mockingly. "Just let me get my coat, and I'll be with you. We can have a merry evening together discussing your inferiority complexes."

They ate at Daisy's in the Kings Road, sharing a large

round table with several other people. But as it was some office party and had been on the go for some time, they were left in relative peace.

"It was pretty mean of you to let me ramble on the last time we met. You must know the diplomatic scene backwards," Pringle said sternly towards the end of the meal.

"Oh don't let's talk about that. I've had diplomacy in a big way these days, I can tell you. Non-stop conferences and round the dinner-table discussions about the American situation, about oil, about the Middle East."

"What shall we talk about then?" he said, ordering a second bottle of the red wine of the house. He had had more than his share of the first bottle.

"What shall we talk about then?" she parroted. "I'll tell you. I like you in some strange way, so let's talk about that."

"Terribly wide subject."

"All right. Let's talk about sex."

"Action, not words."

"Very well," she said. "Let's have action, and our table companions are becoming too noisy for my mood. Take me home to bed."

Rapid, but he could hardly object.

They lay back in his large Victorian bed. Six foot wide Victorian beds don't come that often and he was proud of it. Clothes seemed to be scattered in every corner of the room. What had happened had happened for the third time about an hour previously. They were both feeling quite pleased about that, and they were now lying back on piles of pillows he had gathered together, sipping ice-cold orange juice. They had gone on to that from several whiskies drowned deep in water. It was three in the morning and the next day was Saturday.

Pringle was relaxed and not at all sleepy. Helen lay across him; the tail of a sheet over her hid nothing of note. Her eyes were closed but she was not sleeping either.

Without opening her eyes, she said: "D'you want me to go?"

"Certainly not. Are you expected back?"

"Father's given up, and in any case he's up in Glasgow launching a ship."

"More of a family?"

"Mother died about four years ago. Very high society. I hardly ever saw her. I've got a brother studying law in Berlin."

"And you've had the diplomatic life have you?"

"You're telling me! Uprooted every three or four years, no home life. Parents seen for a few minutes between them coming in at the end of a day in the Embassy or after some dreadful women's tea party, then rushing off to receptions, cocktail parties and dinners. Shipped off to boarding schools, and now as I reach maturity and should escape, my father expects me to act the little hostess for him the whole time. Weeks on end I spend the evening sitting beside the most boring people you can imagine."

"You meet the famous. I have my own humble experience of that from Embassy life abroad."

"The famous are ninety-five per cent boring too. They've made it, they keep telling you they've made it, then they stop trying, except for the occasional dirty old man who's got something else on his mind."

"Dirty young men are more fun?"

"You are anyway."

"Thanks love. Come again."

"Again?"

They drove leisurely homewards at six on a fine, slightly misty London morning. She was worried that the Residence staff might start gossiping, and her father sometimes rang her first thing when he was away on trips. The streets were almost deserted. Two or three electric milk carts, a man sweeping Lambeth Bridge, a few policemen round Westminster, stamping and swinging their arms against the cold. An ambulance, blue lamp flashing, spun by on its way to St Thomas's Hospital. A cheerful group of elderly women cleaners bustled along, bound for the green and cream Treasury and Foreign Office buildings. Up Whitehall and a Guardsman peered out through the closed gates of Horse Guards. Pigeons were rising and fluttering around Nelson's Column. They drove along the Mall and up past Green Park. The German Ambassador's Residence was in Belgrave Square.

"I can't tonight. There's some cultural evening I promised father I'd go to. How about Sunday?" she said suddenly.

He hadn't thought ahead. He had been enjoying the time as it went along, but knew that what suited her would suit him.

"I hadn't asked you yet, but I'll just manage to wait," he said as they parked the car. "Come for lunch tomorrow, or we'll go out somewhere."

"And you'll send me away at three-thirty? Well brought up diplomats always leave luncheons by three-thirty."

"If you insist, and are very good, you can stay on."

"Aren't I very good?"

"You're very good."

She smiled sweetly, kissed his cheek seductively, and at the same time brought her hand across just short of its destination.

"Do that again and father's phone call or not, backstairs gossip can go to hell and I'll abduct you."

"Oooo ... lovely," she said teasingly as she got out of the car. "Forcibly I hope. I'll be at your flat about midday. Bye." She shut the door, waved and disappeared towards the door of the Residence. He slipped the car into gear and drove off in a tired but pleasant frame of mind. And it was Saturday, too, so he could go straight back to bed and get some sleep. With Helen around he was going to need to conserve energy.

Seven o'clock and he was home in the flat, but he was not very sleepy and as he arrived back at the same time as the small West Indian newspaper boy who had the most rousing whistle in the whole of South London, he settled down with more orange juice and a coffee to work his way through *The Times*.

There was an article by the paper's Washington correspondent reporting speculation as to a change of American Ambassador in London. Two or three names were mentioned. One was a career man, but generally the correspondent's conclusion was that the usual procedure of giving plum jobs to strong party backers would happen again. The favourite name was that of ex-Senator Henry A. Middleton. At the bottom of page two there was a short report on the launching at Upper Clyde Shipyards of an advanced design of container ship by the German Ambassador. It was the first of three to be built there for a German company, and it marked, so the story had it, yet one more lease of life for the Upper Clyde yard.

In the Saturday magazine section there was a long article on the British who had supported Hitler up to the beginning of the war. He read that on September twelfth, 1939, a group of prominent men met in London following the outbreak of the war. The manifesto the group had read to them had been prepared by one of the foremost English Dukes, a man who had been a life-long friend of Churchill himself. The document praised Hitler as a man who "flung down the systems by which the international financier—who is an exploiter, never a producer—has accumulated his wealth and power". The group aimed at persuading Chamberlain to make far-reaching concessions to Hitler in order to end the war, avoid the situation where "the two races ... which are the most akin and the most disciplined in the world will continue hostilities until both are bled almost to death". Among the Peers and Members of Parliament there were a number of well-known names. There were names in the article, well-known names from the past. It became more interesting when it talked about people now in positions of power in the country, in Parliament, in industry and the City, but here no names were given. He thought of Sir Geoffrey Benner. Well he could relax now.

CHAPTER TWELVE

Foreign and Commonwealth Office, London, S.W.1

PRINGLE HAD INVITED a friend who was in Consular Department to join Helen and himself for lunch, having extracted a promise from him that he would not outstay his welcome. In the event he woke Pringle at ten-thirty on the Sunday morning saying that he would not be able to make it. Spain was his territory, Celtic had been playing Reàl Madrid the previous afternoon, and there were something like two hundred penniless Celtic supporters camped out on the steps of the Embassy in Madrid, not to mention about forty locked up in various Spanish gaols all over the city in the aftermath of an evening away from the accustomed whisky, but spent plentifully on cheap Spanish wine. Pringle's friend was in the office for the whole day. He might drop around later for a drink. Pringle said better not. He might not be in.

Pringle knew how some of these Celtic supporters must feel. He had gone to a wild party an architect friend had given the previous night in his top floor studio just off the Kings Road. There had been an extremely potent champagne cocktail which he should, from previous experience, have remembered to keep clear of. What the man's architecture was like Pringle had little idea, but his champagne cocktail was powerfully constructed. He had left his car and taken a taxi when he realised he was having difficulty in inserting the key in the door lock. At one stage in the evening he had come across a physiotherapist who danced like a limpet and would certainly have collaborated. But he was still recuperating and had better things in store for the next day. Much better things. Very much better things. He remembered going through a romantic and then maudlin stage about Helen before the drink blurred his better feelings into more basic ones.

Ten-thirty and she was coming at twelve-thirty or thereabouts. First requirement was to get rid of the headache. He put on a jersey and a pair of old corduroys and ran the three hundred yards to the underground station, bought the Sundays and then ran home again, stopping only to buy some eggs and a loaf at a little shop that never seemed to shut. Back at the flat his headache was worse than ever. But the aspirins, a shower, some cold tonic water from the 'fridge and two cups of coffee made him feel a lot better. He tidied the house and sorted out the lunch. They were dining in he had decided.

A good additional reason, or excuse for that was that it had started to rain torrentially, and his car was two miles away in Chelsea. She could drive, but he never found Sunday lunches out very agreeable. So he had bought steaks, salad, cheese and fruit, and there was still some quite reasonable burgundy in the broom cupboard where he kept his wine. Preparations made, he settled down with the *Sunday Times*. They, too, had a back page piece on who the new US Ambassador might be. There was apparently a filmstar in the running as well. Pringle had never heard of him.

By twelve-thirty he was quite excited. By twelve-forty-five he was up and down looking out of the window every few moments. By one o'clock he had decided that she wasn't going to turn up, and five minutes after that had added the conclusion that she had never intended to come. The rain poured down and he decided against phoning her home and in favour of beginning to cook the steaks. At one-thirty she arrived, very wet but remarkably cheerful.

"It's the first time I've been late for anything in years," she said. "Sorry to have begun on you."

"Don't you have ... didn't you come by car?"

"Carburettor's gone funny. I know about cars, and it wasn't firing properly, so I decided on the bus. Such is my status in life that I don't do that very often." She laughed. "I worked out the route. A bus door-to-door more or less, except that I discovered that they don't run often on a Sunday morning, and the first one I took stopped at Victoria. Then it wasn't quite door-to-door this end, at least the way I came. I think I got a bit lost."

"Not to worry. Have a brandy. You're soaked."

"A good excuse for taking my clothes off," she said, and then promptly did just that. All of them, and in the middle of his study. He went to the window and adjusted the Venetian blinds. There was a lady across the road who was permanently stationed behind her net curtains, and it might spoil her Sunday thoughts.

"Brandy?" he asked. He was in the mood already.

"Mmm. Yes please," she said, coming up to him and curling his arms around her. "That's better. I do love the sensation of heavy sweaters when there's nothing to get in the way between them and me. Have you a dressing-gown I can borrow?"

"Towelling or silk? But must you?"

"Bit chilly, though the room's warm. Let me adjust around this brandy first. Oh, towelling please. Not-too-soft towelling, smelling of hot baths, after-shave and men."

"You get worked-up about cloth don't you? Towelling and woollens and so on."

"You can't talk about getting worked-up!" She laughed, moving away from him. "See, now I've embarrassed you."

"I'll get the dressing-gown," he said, darting from the room.

On his way back he stopped to turn down the potatoes. By the time he got back she had put on a record and was trying to light the logs in the fireplace.

He threw her the dressing-gown and she wrapped it

round herself, expertly leaving appetite-whetting glimpses of her figure.

"I haven't had the fire on for ages. Smokeless zone and a hell of an effort to clear out, and it smokes a bit too. But just for you..." He went to the basket and picked up a firelighter and some kindling.

"Goody," she said, bending over him as he worked. He felt her doing something to the back of his neck.

"The trouble with you, Helen, is that you've got your priorities all mixed up. The three 'Fs'—fire, food and ... what was the other thing?"

"With me, the other thing, as you so rudely called it, comes first. With me and you together, that is."

"Very well," he said, putting the wood down.

"*Very* well?" she mimicked.

"*Very.*"

"Oh Christ, the bloody potatoes."

"How domestic." She uncurled herself. "Potatoes eh? Watch your figure. A man of your age..."

He tapped her gently across the part of her that was nearest to his free hand.

"Mmm. Lovely. More."

"The potatoes, Helen. Burnt solid, I bet."

"You'll make someone a beautiful husband. I must pass the word around. Ow! Gosh that was mean. All right, if your potatoes are more important to you than I am..."

"It's not just that, it's the pot as well. Ruined, at a guess. And the stove."

"Just for a handful of cinders he left her..."

"How literary you are. We'll talk Browning later if you like. I'm going to the kitchen." He grabbed his corduroys and made an undignified exit. The pot was badly charred.

Helen came into the kitchen as he poured cold water over the blackened mess. It hissed and spat. "Nasty smell," she said, "but you British could never cook."

He put the pot down and dealt with her. She broke away and ran into the bedroom laughing, the dressing-gown streaming from her shoulders behind her. It was five o'clock before they had the steak and salad.

Perfectly timed, they were wondering what to do next but both were rather exhausted by one prospect, when the phone rang.

Helen had just said, "I think we'll have to employ a chaperone to keep us apart. It must be bad for the heart or something."

"Or something," he replied, and picked up the receiver. "Yes, who's that?"

"Resident Clerk here. Gilbert Winter would like you to come in please."

"Oh bugger. When? Now? Not straight away? Really, I can't. I have half a dozen old aunties visiting..." He listened for a moment or two. "OK. Just a minute," he said eventually, and putting his hand over the mouthpiece told Helen.

"How long," she asked.

"Two hours maximum."

"May I stay?"

"I was intending to lock you in."

"No need. Daddy's gone on to Edinburgh and the staff has today and tomorrow off, and I've left my receiver off."

"You plan, don't you."

"When I want something, yes."

"Hello, hello, are you still there?" The irritable voice of the Resident Clerk reminded him of the receiver in his hand.

"In half an hour then," he said. "Oh no, three-quarters of an hour. I have to pick up my car first."

He phoned for a taxi and while waiting for it he got Helen established in a hot bath, with towels, things to read and drink, and showed her how to work the tape deck. He started to look for some clothes for her, but she protested that the bathrobe was quite good enough until her own clothes, which they had sadly neglected during their other preoccupations, dried out.

The rain had lessened, and the sky was that yellow colour, heavy and threatening, which makes one long to be inside again. He found his car and drove in to Westminster, parking in the Foreign Office courtyard. Out of hours the gate under the archway was the only one open. He showed his pass to the guard. "Good evening Mr Wilson," he said. Pringle made up his mind to correct the man, if he had time and energy, on his way out.

"Miserable one," he answered. "Resident Clerk called me in. I'll just go up." He made his way towards the lift.

"I wouldn't bother going all the way up, Sir. It's Mr Winter wants to see you. He said there was someone coming in. He's in his first-floor office." Pringle nearly asked the guard what was amiss. He might even know.

He went up the one flight to Winter's office and went in. He was there with Terry Miller and another man whom he did not know.

"Sorry to drag you away from your aunties," Winter gave a brief smile. "Charity work on Sundays. Very good indeed." They all laughed.

"This is Peter Halley." They shook hands. Pringle knew the name, though not the man, and he knew what he did. He was the political counsellor in the Washington Embassy and reputed to be a high flier, as future success material is called in the Service.

Winter wasted little time in explaining. Halley had sent him a letter through the bag which had arrived late on Friday, covering the material which had originated from Ed Macartney, the Assistant Secretary at the State Department who had recently committed suicide. As soon as he had got the letter, he had sent a telegram requesting that Halley come home for consultations.

"Peter arrived this afternoon and has to leave again

first thing tomorrow morning," Winter went on. "That's why we have to have this meeting tonight. He's got a lot to tell us; we have some background to feed into him to pass on to the Ambassador in Washington, and at a stage like this, sending letters and telegrams back and forward is no substitute."

"To summarise the political situation," Winter continued rapidly, "the White House, according to all our information, has decided to follow the Mainfare line. They intend to play it tough, on the withdrawal, on the US bases, and at the same time the economic pressures are to be stepped up. New economic measures are to be introduced which will give more support to American firms operating in Eastern Europe and the developing world, and there's going to be a hell of a stink in the commercial world. At the same time we are certain they are just about to nominate a new man to London. We expect to have his name put to us for the Queen's Agrément perhaps tomorrow. How do we react?"

"Are we certain that only the one man is in the running," Pringle asked. "I see the press have two or three names to bandy about."

"As far as we were aware," Peter Halley said, "there were only three real candidates. Ed Macartney would have been a great choice as far as we are concerned. A lot of us knew him from the time when he was Minister at the US Embassy here a few years ago. Despite the fact that no Administration likes the plum jobs going to Career men, rumour has it that he was offered the job and then, under pressure from Mainfare, they changed their minds because he was too honest, too loyal to the Atlantic partnership ideals. He would not have wanted to be their puppet front man in any case."

"That's enough to make a man commit suicide?" Winter asked.

"I don't think so. He was a balanced sort of fellow. I

met him once or twice and it's difficult to believe. But I hear that he had cancer and was dying in any case."

"Who else?" Pringle interrupted.

"Well, presuming there isn't a dark horse, and everything is possible, there is also the heart-throb actor Dale Friend. He put a lot of money behind the Party and he's looking for his reward. But I can't believe even Mainfare would give him any support, because he's a fool. He made a complete gaffe yesterday, according to the Reuter tapes, and couldn't even get our Prime Minister's name right. So that leaves number three."

"Ex-Senator Henry Middleton. What's he like?" Pringle asked.

"I've not met anyone who really knows," said Peter Halley. "Middleton is a strange man. On the plane I scribbled down on a piece of paper a personal assessment of him from what was previously known. You can read it at your leisure. The main point is that he is an old college friend of Mainfare, and he's part of the deal being made with the President. He's got a good enough record admittedly, and his family fortunes have been more than generous in support of the Party. In Congress and in the Senate he was and is respected, and there are even those who think he is no fool, that only very clever deceptions in his party organisation plus a basic trust in some of his personal staff let him down and brought about his electoral defeat. They have been looking about for favours to give him, for something to reward him that would match his ability and be a measure of his past and future use to the Party. A month ago Middleton was reported to have been called to the State Department from where he emerged pleased. A few days later he was called to the White House and emerged delighted. There has been a lot of press speculation. To be American Ambassador at the Court of St James is still a large plum," Peter Halley concluded, "and in my opinion Middleton will get it, if we agree."

"Most useful," Winter said. "Thank you, Peter. Now where do we go from here? That is all more or less public knowledge. Let's see how this new evidence affects matters. It is dramatic in its way, but as an accusation, does it hold water?"

"What does it amount to?" he went on. "There are a series of photostats of letters, two photographs, one old, one quite modern; there is the photostat of a passbook, a German SS Officer's passbook; there is another photostat of an international transfer credit note from a Swiss bank, for a very large amount of money indeed; there is the deed number relating to the title to a house and estate in Pennsylvania; and there is a carefully reasoned and almost convincing document which, backed up by the documentary evidence, suggests that Wilhelm Schenker, SS Lieutenant and a man who until April 1945 was a junior *Aide-de-Camp* to Adolf Hitler, the Führer of the Third Reich, is one and the same as ex-Senator Henry Middleton, the man who, in all likelihood is about to be named as United States Ambassador at her Majesty's Court of St James'."

"So where does all this get us," Winter repeated. "It's late I know, but we've got to make up our minds now while Peter is still here. Peter knows Johnnie's mind too." Johnnie was Sir John Rankine the Ambassador in Washington, a tough individual who believed in the so-called traditional values, but also believed in using modern methods to further them.

"If they put his name forward tomorrow, then we'll have to recommend that the Palace refuse Agrément. It'll cause a lot of fuss and will leak out to the press in no time," Halley said.

"Unprecedented, but what the hell," added Terry Miller. "A good kick in the teeth may do them a little good. I wonder when was the last time we refused to accept an Ambassador?"

"I'll ask Protocol in the morning," Pringle said. "We'll need it for the Submission."

"Then the problem is how to obviate the fuss, is that it?" asked Winter slowly. "Is that all it really amounts to? For example, do we tell the Americans all or only a part of what we suspect? Even if it's true, what good does that do? It knocks their man out, but then they come up with someone else. The Secretary of State isn't going to like that sort of advice. And he'll have to say something in the House."

"Excuse me for asking," Pringle said, "but why don't we go ahead and grant the man Agrément? They may come with his name tomorrow, but nothing more will happen for quite some time. The present Ambassador's got to have time to pack up, and that will take a month or two."

"Your exertions with your aunts have obviously taxed your strength," Winter said dryly. "You miss the point. We're wondering how to sell the refusal to grant Agrément."

"You'll brand me as an angry young man, Gilbert, full of deceit and so on. Old values dead, emulating nasty foreign practice, etcetera, etcetera. But we could be a bit devious for a change," Pringle said. "Perfidious Albion has about as much will to be perfidious as a vicar preaching his sermon or a policeman on the beat. When we occasionally try a tap below the belt, we usually do it out of panic, get our timing wrong, and wait till the eyes of the world are on us. Why not let him in and then hold him down. Could be very useful knowing nasty things about someone."

"Scarcely in the best traditions..." began Winter.

"What best traditions?" said Pringle. Then, "Sorry Gilbert. I didn't mean..."

"Not at all," Winter said. "I was in fact trying to be funny. I've obviously lost the art. I was about to say that the idea isn't totally out."

"Johnnie wouldn't like it," said Peter Halley.

"I'm not so sure. Play them at their own game. Ends justifying the means suit Johnnie more than everyone thinks."

Pringle was very pleased. He had launched the idea, now everyone had picked it up. That was how decisions were born. Stage two, with a man less astute than Gilbert Winter, was to persuade the initially unwilling party that he had thought of it. This time it wasn't the case.

"All right," Winter said. "Just supposing we give him Agrément as you suggest. Get him lunched and launched and then as it were, suddenly discover all this information and use him to put on the screws. Once Hitler's ADC, now Mainfare's: what would happen then?"

"It would depend on how devious we got," Pringle said happily. "Do we then tell the President, or do we just whisper to his Ambassador?"

"Blackmail the Ambassador? Oh we could hardly do that," said Peter Halley.

"I fail to see the difference in moral terms," Pringle said. "Blackmail is blackmail. I wonder when we last used that as an instrument of policy. I doubt Records won't be able to give me an answer on that."

They left it there, with no final decision taken. Pringle was to do a draft, putting forward the various possibilities. The others would 'see how it looked'. Halley was to get it telegraphed to him, for his personal eyes only. At that moment Pringle was clear in his own mind how he would phrase the Submission but it had all changed by the time he set pen to paper.

It was three hours later that he got away and went back to the flat. He was home in six minutes, which was fast going, given the wet roads. The rain had stopped.

He let himself in with the latch key. The house was in silence and at first he thought she had gone. But she was in bed with the side light on, an empty glass beside her, and magazines and the day's newspapers strewed across the bed. Her mouth was closed, her hair hung down one cheek and on to her shoulder. She still wore his bathrobe which was open down the front. She looked beautiful and he felt something in him that had not happened for a long time. And lust it was not. He took his jacket off and carefully lay down on the bed beside her. She stirred, put her arm across and held him.

"Welcome home," she said sleepily.

"My goodness, I feel it," he said. "You make me feel at home even though you are an Ambassador's daughter."

"Someone has to be," she said, and she opened her eyes and looked at him. "It's a real disadvantage in life but someone has to be."

CHAPTER THIRTEEN

Foreign and Commonwealth Office, London, S.W.1

THE SECRETARY OF State had a rather untidy bandage round his left index finger. Pringle wondered how he had done it. They were standing in his room on the first floor of the North West corner of the Foreign Office building, waiting for the German Ambassador to arrive. Pringle stood apart from the others, staring out at the trees in St James's Park. In the distance a military band was playing, and from much closer came the sound of a horse's hooves rising clearly above the noise of the traffic. He looked at his watch: five to eleven, and the Brigade of Guards' subaltern was riding past on his way from Wellington Barracks to mount the guard at Horse Guards. He had seen him so often, lonely and outdated amid the hooting taxis, until he came into his own at the colourful little ceremony under the eyes of the ever-present mass of tourists.

Cabinet had decided that the evidence against Middleton was too slim, whether or not they eventually granted Agrément. The PM had subsequently ruled that the Germans were to be consulted and that Sir Geoffrey Benner should be called to task. This was the first step.

Besides the Secretary of State, there were three in the room: Gilbert Winter, the Principal Private Secretary with whom Pringle had spoken from the Resident Clerk's flat, and Pringle was there to take a record. One of the Assistant Private Secretaries was at the Ambassador's entrance at the back of Downing Street waiting for the German Ambassador. He was due at eleven and would be precise.

"Cut myself trying to sharpen a coloured crayon for my grandson," the Secretary of State broke the silence and beamed round at them. Pringle found it difficult to imagine him doing anything as mundane as sharpening a child's pencil, though he knew the Minister had his private life. It was well publicised in the press through his wife's outspoken behaviour on matters of public interest. He was a moderately distinguished-looking man with a popular public image. He had not put a foot wrong since he took office eight months previously, and had adapted well and to the workings of diplomacy both inside and outside the Foreign Office. He accepted the advice of his officials, something always welcome to career diplomats, but not blindly, which earned him a degree of respect. And he could be firm in putting the Office's views to Whitehall and in Cabinet. The Office liked a strong but pliable minister. They also liked a man who would read the briefs, someone who would keep to them when it came to negotiating. A bit of extra temperament did not matter too much either. He added flair, a touch of the unusual which always went down well with foreigners, or so conventional wisdom had it. It certainly went down well with foreign diplomats. Someone erratic and unpredictable was good cocktail party material.

The Assistant Private Secretary put his head round the door. "The Ambassador has arrived, Secretary of State."

"Good. Bring him in. Gilbert, any last minute advice?" The Foreign Secretary always called his senior officials by their Christian names.

"No, Sir. I don't think so. It's all in the brief. The idea is not to give too much away, but at the same time to give the Ambassador the message that we have something hard to go on and that we want any confirmation he can give. Lay on the delicacy of the whole business."

"Quite," said the Secretary of State, as the German Ambassador was ushered into the room.

"Good morning, Werner. Sorry to drag you in like this." First names were the score here too. In London diplomatic society one had arrived when that happened. If an Ambassador were plain Your Excellency, then he was yet to have made his mark. On the other hand, the Ambassador knew that the informality was one-sided and Ministers were Ministers.

"Not at all, Secretary of State, not at all." Werner Kuhl spoke immaculate English. He was a small man with thinning, swept-back hair, and his suits were as tailored as his English accent. He wore a New College tie, and a long time ago he had even been to Eton until the war broke out. He had brought with him his First Secretary whom Pringle knew slightly from Brussels days, Walter von Sattendorf, a man recently arrived from Bonn. They all shook hands, the Secretary of State carefully introducing everyone, including Pringle, by name. He had briefed himself even on that before the meeting; it showed the care he took.

"Von Sattendorf rang your Private Office to find out what you wanted to see me about," the Ambassador began. "I take it it's about the US withdrawal?"

"Yes, I'm sorry we couldn't be more precise on the phone. It is to do with the Americans in a way. We've picked up one or two bits and pieces of information which hang together into something which could be embarrassing, but at the same time could be helpful to the European position. Trouble is it's not the sort of thing we would want to make public. A little silent investigation if you like; that's why I've called you in. It's an unusual request, and I'd hate the press to get hold of it. Just the sort of thing *Der Spiegel* loves."

"Can you be a little more explicit, Secretary of State?"

"A man has come to our attention ... the details I won't trouble you with. But he appears to have had a past, if you see what I mean."

"A Nazi past?"

"How clever of you Werner. Yes, something like that.

He's now an American citizen."

"Could we have his name? Take a note von Sattendorf."

"His name now won't be much help to you. He was called Wolfgang Schenker. I understand he was on the staff in the Führerbunker right up until the end. We wonder if you could let us know what happened to him." Pringle frowned slightly; the Secretary of State had got the man's name wrong.

"Rather an unusual request, as you say, Secretary of State. You know that the Russians or the Allies took nearly all the records that were available. You hold many still in the Berlin Documentation Centre: there is masses of stuff in Washington. I am sure your own archives are bulging with papers, and of course the Russians have the rest. Why do you ask us?"

"We've gone through all this, Werner. There's no possibility of approaching the Russians or the Americans on this case, and we have already discreetly gone through the papers in our own possession and in Berlin. We know that your government does have a considerable quantity of Third Reich documents in its keeping. We would like you to do a very rapid trace for us."

"Why yes, of course. But I am still not quite sure, if you'll forgive me saying so, Secretary of State, why you called *me* in to tell me all this. There are other ways, more routine ways between our police forces and security services which could do this. I won't say that it happens every day, but there must be fairly frequent checks and cross-checks of each other's records."

"Yes, quite. I understand your doubts, Werner. But political factors are involved. Another consideration is time. We are under this threat of a massive American withdrawal from Europe. We are equally threatened, as you are, by the proposed economic policies of the American Government. This is a small straw of information. We don't know where it is going to lead. But it is a report, from a source too surprising to discount—you will forgive me if I don't breach confidences and tell you what the source actually is, but you can take it it's an excellent one—high up in American ... er ... political circles—which told us that a certain major personality in our relations with the United States spent some of his early days in the Führerbunker."

"But, again, forgive me for saying so, Secretary of State, but that was thirty years or so ago. Not everyone in that Bunker was a guilty man. They were not warders from Belsen or Dachau. We are perhaps all guilty—a mass guilt if you like, but even if this man did have some past in the ruins of the Berlin Chancellery, what crime is that that could help solve our present problems? And quite apart from that, this man, this man Wilhelm Schenker, must have been someone very junior indeed, a nonentity. And even they have been more or less all accounted for, right down to Hitler's valets and chauffeurs. Your newspapers from time to time find Martin Bormann and so on living in South American jungles, but this aside..." The Ambassador laughed.

"Quite so, Werner. But we would still be grateful if you could check. You see we found a trace of a man with the same name in some of our Military Government papers in 1945 and 1946, and we think he was around even later. I have a dossier of what we know. I would be grateful for your assistance, and..." the Secretary of State paused, "the greatest possible discretion."

"Of course, of course, my dear Secretary of State." The Ambassador was irritated and seemed far from convinced. "I will take it up immediately."

"We have a team ready to fly to Germany to help if this should be required. As I said, speed is of the essence."

"The team I think will not be required. I shall set enquiries in motion at once. But I expect little will come of it all. It was all such a long time ago," the Ambassador repeated with a trace of theatrical sadness in his voice.

The two men stood up; they walked to the window talking about other more general political matters. Pringle went over and pulled both the Principal Private Secretary and Gilbert Winter into a corner.

"What's the matter?" the PS said crossly. "I can't leave that Sattendorf chappie standing by himself."

"But this is important," Pringle said. "The Secretary of State made a mistake. He gave the man's name as Wolfgang Schenker."

"So bloody well what? If you've done your preparation properly the correct name and details are all in the dossier we're handing over." The PS was angry. Winter looked at Pringle strangely.

"Exactly," Pringle said. "But the German Ambassador hadn't seen the dossier then. The Secretary of State called him Wolfgang, the Ambassador gave the man his correct name, Wilhelm."

"A slip of the tongue," said the PS.

"Are you positive?" Gilbert Winter asked.

"Absolutely," Pringle replied. "I've been living with these papers, don't forget. And von Sattendorf looked pretty uneasy too."

"Then a slip of the tongue, as I said," responded the PS.

"A strange one," Pringle muttered. It was his turn to be irritated.

"Maybe you're right," Winter said. There was a pause. The PS looked thoughtful, walked over to von Sattendorf, made some sort of apology, and then came back and joined the others again. The Secretary of State and the Ambassador were still ignoring the rest, locked in deep conversation by the window overlooking Horse Guards.

"All right," said the PS. "It's the sort of thing the Minister will try and will enjoy doing. I'll tell him. He may want to play it before the Ambassador leaves."

After a few moments, the Secretary of State led his visitor back from the window and the latter made as if to leave. Gilbert Winter made a deliberate set at the Ambassador with a question about the next Anglo-German Königswinter Conference, and about who was to attend from the British side. Pringle watched the PS buttonhole the Secretary of State with an expertise that comes of experience. He whispered urgently in his ear. The Secretary of State's face reflected first doubt, then something approaching amusement. In the end he nodded.

He went across to where the Ambassador was talking to Winter. Von Sattendorf was standing in the background watching, realising something was afoot.

"Well, thank you again for coming in, Werner."

"No trouble, Sir."

"And you'll let us know what you've found out about our friend Wolfgang or Wilhelm Schenker. I'm told I made a slip earlier over the name. Thank you for correcting me, Ambassador. It's a pleasure to deal with someone who knows his subject."

The Secretary of State gave what could only be described as a giggle, at the Ambassador's obvious discomfiture. His Aide looked ill at ease.

"Don't worry, Werner. I didn't mean to trap you. It was a genuine mistake, and—in a way I would have been more surprised if you didn't know, if the man's name hadn't been familiar to you. Why don't you go and get your government's clearance to discuss the whole thing with us?"

The Ambassador looked shaken. His professional veneer had been punctured and in front of his subordinate at that. A mistake was a mistake. It might not matter in the long run, but the Ambassador did not like to be made to look a fool.

The Secretary of State gripped his hand. "Look Werner, it was my mistake in the first place. It was this lad who picked it up." He pointed at Pringle and laughed.

The Ambassador shot an icy glance at Pringle, said his goodbyes, shaking hands pointedly only with Winter and the PS, and then left the room escorted by von Sattendorf and the Private Secretary, with a "Goodbye Secretary of State. We shall certainly be in touch".

The door shut behind them. The Secretary of State turned to Pringle and said: "Well done, and very observant of you. I don't know if it will help, but I enjoyed doing it. Werner is a bit of a stuffed shirt. But I'm not sure if he'll forgive you making a fool of him in a hurry."

"No sir," Pringle said quietly. That was the least of his worries then.

When he had finished dictating a record of the meeting, Pringle turned to two reports that had come in, one of an interview with Benner, and the other with a man named Coles. He was a character whose name had appeared on the Library files as a former Nazi sympathiser, and as there was a recent report about him as well, it had been agreed to try to discover what he knew.

Secret and Personal Report by an un-named official of two interviews conducted at an address in Lower Regent Street at 1030 hrs and 1500 hrs on Tuesday 5th December 1972

Benner, Sir Geoffrey Charles, TD, MP for Cronedale (West), born 1902 in Basingstoke. Entry in *Who's Who* basically correct. Missing details include early wartime spent in Stockholm, reputedly as freelance journalist, but see British Embassy Report CY-1995 of 15 June, 1942, and subsequent minuting (attached as Annex A), which suggests treasonable or at best pacifist activities. Latter hardly borne out by later war and reservist record which was good. Proceedings not instituted for lack of evidence at the time. 1945: case papers officially closed.

At beginning of interview subject was extremely difficult and abusive over method used to bring about meeting (called in to meet visiting American real estate man). Newly available evidence of early war activities was therefore used which produced reluctant co-operation in return for promise of no embarrassing revelations.

Subject shown available biographical material on Wilhelm Schenker including photographs (items D731/5) dated 1942, 1944, 1953 and 1971. Subject understood the relevance at once. Was prepared to substantiate identity of person in 1942 and 1944 photographs as Wilhelm Schenker: was also reluctantly prepared to admit similarity of person in 1953 photograph. Refused point blank to commit himself over relevance of 1971 print, even when under pressure. Was obviously shocked by this trend in the interrogation.

Subject said he was unable to throw further light on war time or subsequent activities of Wilhelm Schenker and claimed that he had believed he had been killed in Berlin in the last fighting in 1945. He had met him on three, perhaps four, occasions only. He understood his role to have been personal assistant rather than secretary or ADC. There were better-known individuals filling these latter rôles. Subject claimed to have no knowledge of any of the personalities involved after 1942.

Subject was then confronted with the recent intelligence gained from 1946 Foreign Office files, the diary and the Macartney material. His reaction was unco-operative. He subsequently refused to say anything further, and the interview was concluded some ten minutes later, subject indicating that he would be consulting his lawyers.

Comment: Although subject threatened legal proceedings, it is extremely unlikely that this will be carried out due to nature of enquiry. Despite initially arrogant demeanour, subject was aware of what investigations threatened for his political reputation, and was shaken by course of interview. A strong impression remains that he knows at least some more, and, considering his age and position, further interview later may still produce better results.

Coles, Adrian, born 1907 in Cheam. Preparatory School teacher (classics). Excused military service on medical grounds. (Home Guard.) Unmarried, two incidents with boy pupils 1933 and 1937. Second led to unsuccessful criminal prosecution: case dismissed for lack of evidence. Briefly interned due to year's membership (1938) of Mosleyites. No other biographical information immediately available, but investigations are continuing.

After Coles was confronted with latest intelligence regarding the evidence from the Foreign Office files and elsewhere, and with reference made to his recent social indiscretions, he became extremely co-operative. He told us all he knew or had heard about Wilhelm Schenker. In the event not much new emerged, but useful confirmation was gained of the link between the man of the 1953 report and the 1965 to 1971 period. We are now in a position to state with a fair degree of certainty that the individuals to whom these investigations refer are one and the same person. Further documentary evidence, from what Coles said about security methods, in all probability no longer exists.

Comment: Surveillance has been mounted on subject, and will be maintained for a week. Permission has been requested for coverage of his home telephone number for a maximum of ten days. There is a likelihood that, believing he may have spoken freely, his colleagues may attempt to find out what he said, and the extent of the compromise.

Within twenty-four hours this comment was fully substantiated. The next day, by special delivery messenger, Pringle received a transcript of a telephone conversation between Adrian Coles and a caller who did not identify himself.

Date: 5th December. *Time*: 1935 hrs. *Report No.* AF 3509/1.
Coles: Hello? Adrian Coles speaking.
Caller: It's me, Adrian. I rang to check with you. I've been interviewed. Have you?
Coles: Oh God yes. I got a dreadful ... Yes. I tried to contact you to warn you. I left a message at the House for you to ring. Didn't you get it?
Caller: Never mind that. You said nothing I hope. They asked a lot of questions?
Coles: Yes. They knew about Wilhelm. They showed me photographs.
Caller: Recent ones?
Coles: 1971.
Caller: You said nothing?
Coles: No of course I ...
Caller: Good. But they'll be back at you. They're serious. I think I know why, and they'll be back.
Coles: No ... No. I can't stand that. I've got too many other problems. I'm in trouble Ge ...
Caller: In trouble again? Usual thing I suppose, you little creep. Pull yourself together, d'you hear. And say nothing.
Coles: Please understand. Please I can't stand it ... Hello? Hello?

Sir Geoffrey Benner had put the phone down.

Mr Adrian Coles, Kingsmead Castle School

The two small boys, in their neat grey flannel suits, caps rakishly perched on the backs of their heads, left their study dormitories at about six in the evening. Instead of playing rugby they had been working on their Latin prep. They had been kept in for a mixture of reasons; their Latin translations had been poor and, in addition, old Twitcher had suspected correctly that both had had a hand in the derogatory drawing found on the classroom blackboard at the beginning of the lesson that morning. And Twitcher was nothing if not a disciplinarian. 'Little Hitler' was another favourite pseudonym for him among his reluctant pupils.

The two boys, clutching their Kennedy's Latin Grammars and their exercise books, were in no hurry. They loitered as they went down the long path towards the little cottage beside the old coach house at the southern edge of the school grounds. They stopped just out of sight of the school house behind the gymnasium to try out a new catapult, a weapon strongly forbidden at the school, on some unsuspecting blackbird. They were inexperienced and the bird escaped unharmed. One of the senior prefects whistled arrogantly past, casting only a brief glance at the suspicious bulge under the jacket of one of the boys. He might have stopped to investigate, but he would be late for tea, and Matron had promised him cherry cake. Little changed over the years in the simple mentality of the English preparatory schoolboy.

The prefect disappeared from sight, but round the corner came a small, fat little boy. His name was Herring and he suffered terribly at the hands of every bully in the school. The two other boys having failed to wound the blackbird, turned their attention and the catapult's aim at Herring. A round pebble struck rather sharply on the back of a pale chubby knee, and he let out a cry more of fear than pain. He turned and ran as fast as he could away from them in the direction of Twitcher Coles's cottage. Twitcher had shown him some slight glow of sympathy in the past, and Herring was also good at Latin. He had need of an ally, a refuge.

He reached the door, panting and red in the face. His pursuers halted somewhat short of the cottage; the catapult was carefully hidden in some bushes by the side of the path. Herring did not knock or ring but barged straight through the tiny hall and into the living room.

"Sir, Sir," he yelled. "They're after me. They have a cata ... a cata ... a cata ..."

Sir did not answer. He was lying half on, half off, the little couch. His head was thrown back nearly touching the carpet, eyes open, mouth open. White and still. On the floor beside him was a badly torn copy of Gibbon's *Decline and Fall*, a small empty bottle, his broken spectacles and a sheet of notepaper.

Three small boys ran in unity all the way to the headmaster's house. Herring, despite his build, kept up with the other two all the way. It was growing dark and he did not want to be left behind.

Later the Headmaster discussed the matter with the police. Yes, he said, there had been serious complaints. He understood Mr Coles had been in trouble before. A boy had come and told him about Mr Coles's behaviour. He had been intending to discuss the whole matter with the school governors the next day, and Mr Coles would certainly have been sacked even if no criminal charges had been brought. He did not want a scandal. It gave the school a bad name. Yes, he was sure that was why Mr Coles had taken his own life. One could see the forced tension in his writing, quite unlike his usual neat, scholarly hand.

When the two men came down from London the next day, the Headmaster repeated this opinion to them. They came with the Police Inspector; they said they were sure the Headmaster was right. The Headmaster in his turn was far from clear why Mr Coles should be of interest to anyone from London, but he had other things to worry about, and soon forgot his curiosity.

CHAPTER FOURTEEN

Foreign and Commonwealth Office, London, S.W.1

THROUGHOUT THAT WEEK, Pringle was more occupied than he had been for a long time, both by the American crisis which gathered momentum daily, and by Helen who took up more and more of his spare moments. The one did not seem to conflict with the other; he lived, as he said, at a high peak; the adrenalin flowed through him, activity breeding activity. The best of all Parkinsonian models—when he had little to do he did nothing; when overstretched he always managed to fit extra into the day.

On the Tuesday, as anticipated, the Americans asked for Agrément. On the Thursday afternoon, as a contingency measure, documents were prepared to go forward to the Palace for the Queen's approval. The first was the *Note Verbale* from the American Embassy:

> The Embassy of the United States of America presents its compliments to the Foreign and Commonwealth Office, and has the honor to inform that on the instructions of its Government, it is proposed to appoint the Honorable Henry A. Middleton to succeed to the capacity of United States Ambassador at the Court of St James. Details of Mr Middleton's career are enclosed, and the Embassy has the honor to enquire whether his appointment would be acceptable to H.M. the Queen, and to Her Majesty's Government.
>
> The Embassy of the United States of America takes this opportunity to renew to the Foreign and Commonwealth Office the assurances of its highest consideration.

The Note was numbered, dated, stamped and initialled. It would go under a covering submission from the Secretary of State for Foreign and Commonwealth Affairs to the Queen, requesting her Agrément, or in non-diplomatic language, her consent to Mr Middleton's appointment. Pringle prepared the draft.

> The Secretary of State for Foreign and Commonwealth Affairs with his humble duty to Your Majesty, has the honour respectfully to submit for Your Majesty's approval that the Honorable Henry A. Middleton be accepted as Ambassador Extraordinary and Plenipotentiary of the United States of America at Your Majesty's Court.

Whatever the century to which this language might appear to belong, it was planned, if the final decision was taken to recommend Agrément, to send these documents forward from the Foreign and Commonwealth Office, sometime during that month. The Monarch would be spared the less glamorous details about the Ambassadorial candidate. Sometime later the documents would come back. At the top right hand corner of the Secretary of State's submission would be the Royal Cipher. Agrément would have been granted.

The following day brought two pieces of news: first that Adrian Coles had committed suicide, second that Middleton was due to arrive in London over that weekend for consultations. What these consultations were about was not explained by the American Embassy First Secretary who rang up to let the Office know. They were ringing as a matter of courtesy, he explained; ambassadorial candidates did not usually turn up in the country concerned prior to their predecessor's departure, nor were they generally present in between the request for and the granting of Agrément. The Embassy were embarrassed; they hinted that he was coming against their advice, in a purely private capacity, to have a look around and that he would not make any official calls.

This event added urgency to the affair and they now had to get Ministerial agreement on what to do next. Pringle worked on a submission to the Secretary of State, reviewing the evidence of the Library files in the light of material from later German Control Commission files, which showed that between the end of the War and the beginning of the 'fifties, a widespread network of former Nazis and neo-Nazis had been established on an international basis. The leading light in Germany was Professor von Neumann, now a well-established, left-of-centre academic. In Britain, there was Geoffrey Benner, the right wing MP, and in the United States the man who was working, at least when he made his frequent visits back to Germany, under his real name—Wilhelm Schenker. There was also the preparatory school teacher Adrian Coles. His job appeared to have been that of runner or messenger. The world was littered with people who held similar views on politics, race and so on. One less, now that he was dead.

Next, Pringle reported on Dr Pickforth's contribution to the Select Committee's Report: the diary which suggested a major last-minute escape by senior Nazis at the end of the war, plus the cross-references to Benner—and the story Pickforth had brought back from Tel Aviv which added credence to this. Pringle added an element of doubt when he summarised the evidence from Macartney. Macartney was known to have been a frustrated and sick man. Might he not have constructed this evidence as a last twisted revenge? The opinion of people who had known Macartney went to disprove this, but more definite firsthand evidence was needed.

With the exception of the desk work on the Library files, Pringle had done none of the investigation himself. Employees of other branches of the State Machine had gone around interviewing, reporting, following up references and clues. Miller had co-ordinated that side of things. Pringle's task was to précis and synthesise; the amateur drawing conclusions from the work of the professionals.

He wrote the submission on the distinctive blue draft paper. With its broad margin covering a third of its width, that paper is somehow symbolic of the whole way of working which the Foreign Office has inherited and still employs: the check and cross-check. The Desk Officer in the so-called Third Room produces a first draft; his Assistant (in the best traditions this describes a man not his assistant but his immediate superior, the Assistant to the Head of the Department) then works it over, adds his own bubbles of thought into the wide margin and deletes bits that he disagrees with. Then it moves to the Head of Department who amends according to his temperament, personal style and habit. In the meantime copies of the various drafts have been sent to other departments and individuals who might conceivably be interested by the subject, or most importantly by the implications of any given course of action. This well-worked document, the distilled wisdom and wit of many men, is then either typed in final form on stiff blue crested notepaper and signed off by the Head of Department himself, or if very important, it goes on up the ladder to the Under Secretary, to go out above his signature. Too often the end-product is beautifully expressed but wordy, having consumed and digested so many ideas and thoughts and styles in its upward progression.

This particular draft was out of the ordinary. It was of great potential importance, the implications could be very wide-reaching but the sensitivity of the whole exercise was such that as few people as possible were to know about it. While the language used bore little resemblance to Pringle's original draft, the recommendations which Gilbert Winter put forward twenty-four hours later were fairly close to the original. They had decided against perfidy; they proposed that Middleton should be quietly told what they knew about him. They would decide what to do next when they knew how he reacted to the news.

Everyone agreed. The Prime Minister in particular wanted to avoid any further upset to relations with the United States; he accepted that there would be little chance of using Middleton's appointment subsequently to improve the British position through political or personal pressures; but he insisted that before any action was taken, more certain evidence of identity should be found. If Sir Geoffrey Benner were to be used for the purpose, the PM instructed that not too much persuasion was to be applied. A delicate political balance had to be maintained in Parliament and there was to be no witch hunt unless something substantial were to be gained.

Sir Geoffrey Benner, M.P., House of Commons, London

Sir Geoffrey Benner climbed the stairs, walked along the corridor, paused outside one of the oak doors, and then entered the Chief Whip's office. One or two people were in the outer office; were they all deliberately avoiding his eye? He suspected that something must be wrong; he also suspected what it might be. It was some time since he had ben summoned by the Chief Whip.

He went into the inner office without knocking. The Chief Whip was on his own.

"Hello Geoffrey."

"Afternoon, Philip. There was a message that you wanted to see me."

"Yes, that's right, Geoffrey. The PM's asked me to have a word with you."

"What's the matter?"

"Don't really know Geoffrey. It isn't a Party matter and the PM doesn't want it to become one. He's asked me to say how much he hopes there won't be any ... fuss. No publicity or anything like that which might be damaging to the Party. You understand what I'm driving at, Geoffrey? I believe you were talked to in a rather unofficial way the other day. Well, the PM is angry at the way it was handled and you had every right to be annoyed. The officials have been carpeted. But things have apparently gone a stage further now, Geoffrey, and he says he hopes you will be able to help."

"I'm sorry. I don't quite see what you're driving at Philip. What does the PM think ... ?"

The Chief Whip was a powerful man. He was more a do-er than a thinker. He was a disciplinarian and as far as he was concerned what the PM wanted done, was done. He knew his set of rules and expected everyone else to abide by them. He also had been given to understand that Sir Geoffrey Benner would know exactly what he was talking about. There had been rumours of his having instructed his solicitors to take legal proceedings over some interview he had recently been subjected to in the cause of National Security. The Chief Whip was a great believer in National Security. He was right behind the PM when the latter wanted everything settled with no fuss and no publicity. He didn't know the details and he didn't want to. He had other things on his mind. But Party discipline and, in conjunction with the Leader of the Party, the Party's public image, were very much his concern, Sir Geoffrey Benner or no Sir Geoffrey Benner.

"I'm sorry you don't see what I'm driving at Geoffrey," the Chief Whip smiled a smile that had no warmth whatsoever. "As I said, the PM and the Foreign Secretary are most concerned that there should be no fuss. You're in a good safe seat at Cronedale West, Geoffrey. We have a lot of demand for safe seats the way things are going. We don't like them being wasted, if you see what I mean. But I'm sure you do fully understand, Geoffrey. The PM was most insistent that I should make the point to you." The Chief Whip stood up behind his large desk and stared across at the other man. There was a touch of dislike in that look. Sir Geoffrey was the older man, but had never held office. The Chief Whip had a future ahead of him; a future dealing with men and politics, but clean politics. "Sorry I have to rush off now. We're having a little meeting on tactics; how to handle the Immigration Bill Amendments. Could be tricky. I hope this time we'll have your support on them too."

Sir Geoffrey Benner was silent. The Chief Whip had said almost nothing, had not been specific, had talked in conundrums. It would have been an incomprehensible warning to someone who did not know what was being talked about. But Sir Geoffrey did know. Co-operate or else; or else we'll make sure you aren't Sir Geoffrey Benner MP any more. They would find a bright new candidate. It would be easy. The Constituency Association would be dealt with by the Party Central Office. The Chairman would be invited to have lunch with someone important. He might even be seen by the PM. It would all be over in a matter of weeks, buried in the middle of the next General Election which, everyone said, was just around the corner. And would they stop there, at simply taking his seat away from him? He doubted it.

"What do you wish me to do, Philip?" said Sir Geoffrey with controlled anger and what he hoped sounded like a touch of heroics in his voice.

"Pop along and see the Secretary to the Cabinet. PM's asked him to have a word with you. He looks after this sort of in-between stuff. Unwritten, but part of the set-up. Neither politics nor the Civil Service ... eh? Where the whole system meets, locks together. Can you make five o'clock? The PM hoped you'd be able to meet at five, then you will have plenty of time before our three-line whip later this evening. See you then, Geoffrey. I knew you would understand the PM's feeling. See you later." The interview was at an end.

Sir Geoffrey Benner was a hard, well-bred man with all the qualities that go with a politician of the extreme right. He had seldom compromised in his political life, since he had never felt the need nor the inclination to do so. It would be difficult to do so now. But the forces were building up and he was intelligent enough to realise it. It was a situation where some give would be necessary to survive intact in the eyes of the public. For some reason or other, probably associated with Adrian Coles, people had unearthed things about him which had been a long time sleeping. He felt a flash of uncontrolled anger at the thought of Coles. Coles had strong views, and had been useful in the past. He was getting old; his usefulness lay in the past.

Sir Geoffrey went downstairs and along to the Central Lobby. He pushed through the throng of visitors arriving to see their MPs and past the queue of people waiting under the row of statues of former Prime Ministers, to take their turn in the Strangers' Gallery, from where they would consider that they were watching at least the trappings of democracy in action. Down the few steps and across one end of the Great Hall of Westminster, past the two policemen he went and out by St Stephen's Entrance into the hubbub of the beginnings of the London rush hour. More people waiting to go into Parliament; sightseers, Whitehall office staff on their way home; double-decker buses crammed with people; taxis, cars, noise, noise. Sir Geoffrey turned right, past the statue of Cromwell boarded up against possible damage by the excavators of the new underground car park, past the main gates of Parliament itself, with Big Ben towering behind. At the corner of Parliament Square and Bridge Street, the light built into the top of the stone pillar which supported the heavy ornate railings was flashing. It did not signal any dire national emergency, but was only indicating to passing taxis that a Member of Parliament had summoned one.

He crossed Parliament Street and walked up Whitehall past the Treasury, the building housing the Home Office, and then crossed Downing Street to the Cabinet Office. The steel barricade was up across the entrance to Downing Street, and two policemen were checking the passes of people who wished to enter. They were waiting for yet another demonstration. If Sir Geoffrey had had his way, there would be no such demonstrations—ever. They were a negation of democracy, this persistent rabble forcing their turbulent views on the elected government of the country.

The Cabinet Office is housed in part of the Old Treasury Building at No. 70 Whitehall. In the sixteenth century it began life as a recreation area, with the main attraction a cockpit. Sir Geoffrey entered, gave his name to the Security Guard who, having checked his credentials, issued him with a temporary pass and then sent him, with an escort, up in a lift, along a corridor and across a great hall to the Secretary to the Cabinet's office.

Sir Frazer Read was a Scot, one of the very few holders of the high office of Secretary to the Cabinet since the appointment was established during the First World War. Some considered that, after the Prime Minister, he was the single most powerful man in the country, the holder of all the ropes, the channel through which the vast Civil Service and the Parliamentary and Cabinet system of British Government were linked. He was a tiny, dynamic man, exuding strength and, at the same time, charm. Here was no dry faceless Civil Servant. Here was a man who could talk to Kings and keep the common touch with no 'if' about it. He was also a busy man. Immediately they were both seated, and an assistant had come in to take a record, he wasted no words but came to the point at once.

"Sir Geoffrey, I owe you, first of all, an apology for the way you were interviewed recently. The people concerned have been disciplined."

Sir Geoffrey nodded his head slightly but said nothing.

"But you will realise by now that we know a great deal both about your background and about your connections. We have known about them for a very long time; but in the circumstances, it was felt that no action was necessary."

Sir Geoffrey did not need to ask what was being talked about, nor who the 'we' were. He continued to say nothing. He was numbed, more than by his earlier interview, by the realisation that this secret other life had long been far from secret.

"Now things have changed. We are in a dangerous situation in terms of old relationships and alliances. We did not wish to stir things up, Sir Geoffrey. Many things are best left buried and forgotten. The tragic mistakes and follies of the past are part of the history of every one of us." The Secretary to the Cabinet waxed eloquent, stood up and went and stared out of the tall windows which overlooked Horse Guards Parade, ugly under its thick coating of parked cars. There was a rail go-slow and, as usual, the Royal Parks were offering additional free parking space for commuters.

"What do you wish me to do?"

"To identify a man."

"What man?"

"That is for you to tell us. His name used to be Wilhelm Schenker. You met him once, perhaps twice, before the war, Sir Geoffrey, did you not? Then again briefly in 1940? No, do not answer that question. It is irrelevant. In your recent interview you told us about this period. But you claim that you never met him again. We believe, Sir Geoffrey, that this is not the case. You saw him after the War in 1950, perhaps July 1950, and then in 1963. You may also have met him in 1967 sometime shortly after Sunday, August the 13th, 1967. Since then you probably have not met him. You may not, probably do not, know his name now. He is an American citizen, we think an important American citizen."

The Secretary to the Cabinet picked up a buff-coloured file from his desk. It had a blue 'Top Secret' label stuck across the top and bottom. There was no file name or title in the printed box in front that should have contained one. He opened the file and took out two photographs. They were good photographs, studio portraits. One full face, the other taken slightly to the left side.

"Do you recognise him?"

"No."

"Are you sure, Sir Geoffrey?"

"One is never sure. But I do not recognise this man."

"I am disappointed, Sir Geoffrey. I understand your former colleague, Mr Adrian Coles, was much less uncertain. He said, and I quote. 'I cannot be one hundred per cent sure, since many years have passed, but he has the same basic features.'"

"I am at a loss to understand what or whom..."

"Sir Geoffrey, please! I think it would be best for you as well as for us, if you avoided storing up greater embarrassment for yourself. We know all about you. We know that you have seen a certain amount of Mr Coles in recent years, that you telephoned him only two or three days ago to discuss your recent interview with the security authorities."

"And this proves something? I've had enough of this interview. I'm going to see the Prime Minister. I will not be treated like a common criminal."

"Let us hope you will never be treated like a common criminal, Sir Geoffrey. It lies in your hands whether the transcript of your telephone conversation is passed to the police. They may like to examine it in relation to their enquiries as to why Mr Adrian Coles took an overdose of sleeping pills last Thursday evening."

"He's dead?" Sir Geoffrey spoke in a whisper.

"I'm sorry. Yes, he committed suicide. It has not been in the press. It's not a big story and I think it would be a good idea to keep it that way, if you agree. In the national interest, you understand."

There was a pause of some few moments. Sir Geoffrey Benner looked pale and tired. Then he said: "I do not think these are photographs of the man you were talking about." He spoke slowly and softly, choosing each word carefully. The other man in the room, the record taker, had to bend forward and strain to hear what he said.

"Are you sure?"

"I am sure. Almost sure."

"Why 'almost'?"

"Because a man can do great things with his face particularly if he has years of practice, and years to do it in."

"I can show you more photographs."

"That would do no good."

"Then ... ?"

"I would have to see the man. But I am sure you are mistaken."

"Very well. We will arrange for you to see the man." The Secretary to the Cabinet was disappointed.

"When?"

"May I let you know? I understand that he arrived in London this weekend."

"Of course." Sir Geoffrey was shocked for a second time. There was a pause. "But why should you think that, even if this is the man you say I met in the past, even if there were a man and he is not long dead, that I would tell you?"

"We are not sure, Sir Geoffrey. Every man has his loyalties. But if this is the man, then what I am about to say will, I think, persuade you, you who are above all a patriot, even though your patriotism showed a strange and, to many, a grossly unworthy face three decades ago."

"Then tell me, Mr Secretary. Tell me." Sir Geoffrey Benner eased himself back in the deep leather chair. He had regained his composure; he was as relaxed as if he were in his club, as if he had not a care in the world. He prepared to listen.

The black Rover 3000 pulled out of the heavy southbound traffic on Park Lane, and swept up the short approach drive to the main entrance of the London Hilton. It was twenty past six on the twelfth of December. Ten minutes to go before cocktail party time, and a squadron of taxis hustling for position blocked the area. A top-hatted Commissionaire shouted and waved. A space gradually cleared as the taxis unloaded and picked up their fares, and the driver of the Rover pulled into a stretch of open space just beyond the door. Three men got out of the car; the driver stayed where he was and spent the next ten minutes arguing with the Commissionaire whether he could park there. Eventually a policeman was called to settle the matter. The driver said something to the officer, a pass was shown, and the Rover and its driver stayed where they were.

Inside the hall, the camel hair coats and the furs of the rich; a hundred different shades of skin pigment; famous faces and ones that looked as if they should be famous. The three men stood unobtrusively by a glass pillar and prepared to wait.

From half-past six onwards, a steady stream of guests arrived making their way to the lifts and to a reception on one of the upper floors. About a quarter to seven, a fourth man joined the other three. "He's just left the exhibition," he said briefly. "Not long, depending on traffic."

Ten minutes later a large American car pulled up outside the hotel. Somehow the Commissionaire had managed to clear all the taxis and other cars out of its way. The future American Ambassador to London had arrived. The chauffeur opened one door; the Commissionaire opened the other; both saluted. A few people stopped and turned to watch; but only a few people, for important people are commonplace at the Hilton.

Middleton came through the revolving doors and went across to Reception to pick up the key of his suite. An assistant manager recognised him and smiled a standard smile.

One of the three men by the pillar, turned to one of the others: "That's Mr Henry Middleton, Sir Geoffrey."

Sir Geoffrey Benner stared hard at the man who was advancing across the foyer towards the lifts. Middleton was talking to the manager and smiling. The other two men watched Sir Geoffrey equally intently.

When he had disappeared through the lift gates the men turned to Sir Geoffrey. "Well," one of them asked after a short pause. "Was that him?"

Sir Geoffrey Benner looked coldly at the man who had addressed him. "I said, Mr Miller, that I would let the Secretary to the Cabinet know. Let us leave the arrangement as planned, if you please. Now if you would be so kind as to call your car and have me taken back to the House. There is an important foreign affairs debate on this evening in case you are unaware of it." With that, Sir Geoffrey turned and walked towards the door of the hotel and out into the December evening.

CHAPTER FIFTEEN

Foreign and Commonwealth Office, London, S.W.1

THE PRIME MINISTER decided that someone should confront Middleton. There was no question of a Minister doing it; it was too politically delicate. So Gilbert Winter was selected as being of a sufficiently high level, yet not too high; he could be quietly disowned if anything went seriously wrong. Luckless balloon men had been employed before by British governments to test the way the wind was blowing on a particular issue. At first it was decided that no-one else should be present. Later it was considered that there might be a risk in this particular approach; so Pringle went to keep a record. If Middleton objected to a junior diplomat being present, Pringle was to withdraw, and technical means of recording the interview were to be used. Not quite Watergate, but almost.

Of the various ways of setting up the meeting, they opted for the simplest. Winter rang him at his hotel, welcomed him to London and invited him to come in to the office for a chat. Nothing official of course. Middleton reluctantly agreed.

It was a grey day. Pringle was sent down to meet him at the Ambassadors' entrance at the park side of the building, and recognised him at once from his photographs. He smiled agreeably and asked Pringle for his name, a gesture which most people in powerful positions dispense with in their relations with junior aides. Pringle thought Middleton looked too distinguished to fit into the plot. He escorted him up in the Secretary of State's antiquated lift to the first floor. Turning to the left above the gilded main staircase, the most opulent part of the building with

Queen Victoria's forbidding statue at the foot, a display case of King's and Queen's Messenger badges half way up, and at the top, the bust of that most respected of all Foreign Secretaries, Ernest Bevin, Pringle led him through the double doors into Winter's room.

The office furnishings were comfortably Victorian, with a huge desk, deep, rather shabby leather chairs, a large glass-fronted bookcase filled to the top with totally irrelevant bound copies of State Papers going back to the early part of the last century. In front of this Dickensian backcloth, the two men shook hands and sat down facing each other. Pringle, clutching notepad and pencil, perched nervously on the edge of his chair, while Winter's PA brought in three cups of her standard, oversweet, instant coffee which hardly was up to the occasion. Middleton sipped it once and then left it untouched.

Pringle studied both men as they embarked on mutual pleasantries. Middleton, tall, good-looking, fair hair with a touch of grey brushed thickly behind his ears; his high cheekbones gave him a determined, aristocratic appearance which was accentuated by his prominently acquiline nose. He had a warm smile, with a suspicion of hardness behind it. Gilbert Winter, on the other hand, stooping, balding, rimless bifocal spectacles balanced half way down his nose, seemed pedantic and precise, more the popular image of a Treasury man than a suave diplomat. But he, too, had a smile which charmed, all the more because it was unexpected. Both matched up for what must prove to be a unique occasion.

"It was very good of you to suggest I call, Mr Winter." Middleton spoke with a slight transatlantic lilt, a softish voice with no trace of German in it. "I'm sorry I shall be taking up this great appointment at a time when relations are hardly at their warmest."

"Quite so," Winter said reflectively.

"But we cannot expect that relations between two great

peoples will always continue on the same even keel. There are ups; there are downs. We are too, too alike in many ways, we in the United States and you in Britain, and also our friends in Europe. Only the foolish would expect no slight squabbles among the family of nations."

This was hardly a high standard, Pringle thought. It was as if he had learned off by heart some speech to a women's institute.

"Quite so," Winter said again. "But if I may say so, Mr Middleton, on this occasion we in Europe are more than bewildered at the rate with which we are sliding in the downward direction. And I think you will agree that this slide has been brought about more by unilateral action..."

"Europe, Mr Winter, has had it too easy too long," Middleton interrupted. "Too much take, too little give, and too little gratitude. The present Administration is beginning to realise, as its predecessors did not, that generosity breeds contempt. Your people never liked us less than when you were beneficiaries of American post-war aid. Charity brings bitterness and no respect on either side."

"I certainly don't dispute that last remark, Mr Middleton. But there are ways."

"More diplomatic ways, Mr Winter? Is that what you mean? Slow, graceful means? Elegant withdrawal over years? Come, come, Mr Winter. That only prolongs the agony. This way, my way, Senator Mainfare's way, is quick and painful and then it's over. No long, lingering ailment. A quick cut and then we can build afresh on a more equal footing."

"It is one point of view. But you have been talking about American military withdrawal. What about the economic and commercial front?"

"*Laissez faire*, Mr Winter. Free trade is what we need."

"What about the tariff walls, the proposed new tax incentives to American exporters?"

"Economic necessity."

"I would disagree."

"Then let us call it economic self-interest. Every country pursues that policy."

"But is it enlightened economic self-interest? The press are beginning to use the term 'all-out trade war', and it is difficult to disagree with them."

"Well, Mr Winter, I think we know each other's views on this and related problems. It may be a waste of both our times if we rehearse them again here and now."

Middleton looked across questioningly. "You had something more specific to talk about?"

"Yes, Mr Middleton. I am acting on instructions."

"Then it is hardly for that friendly chat, that informal exchange of views that you suggested when you telephoned?"

"No."

"Then, as I suspected, it must be about me?"

"You suspected?" Pringle watched Gilbert Winter suddenly become alert and sit forward in his chair. He was tense. Experienced diplomatic operator though he was, this was something new and out of his experience.

The other man was calm. "I have not lived the life I have over the past thirty years without constantly waiting, constantly suspecting. It has nearly happened three times in that period. I always asked myself why nothing broke, why people did not pursue things right through till they found out the truth. The answer is that they lacked motive, or, as doubtless with my political opponents when I was in the Senate, they lacked the facts."

"And we?" Winter asked quietly, abashed by the man's directness.

"When one is to be appointed as Ambassador to a major nation, a nation, if not one of the very biggest and most important now, certainly one which was in the period we are talking about, one lays oneself open to charges brought by that people. You have a motive and you may have the information. The information, I don't know and hardly care where it comes from. The motive was none of my doing; it was my Government's. When I accepted this appointment, I worked on the presumption that you might know about my history, and that my Government's recent activities might make you use this knowledge. You would not have dug up my past just for my sake."

"So you guessed?"

"I was also informed, and that's why I came over to London to test the water; I heard that enquiries were being made about me; I felt I would give you an opportunity to show your hand. I saw an old colleague Geoffrey Benner at the Hilton Hotel the other day. He was standing with two other men. He saw me, I noticed him, but though we knew each other so well, he did not come forward. I knew that he must have come there for a purpose. I don't blame him. Life is too short, and I should probably have done the same in his place, though I like to think not."

"Then one part of my work is done," Winter said. He looked uncomfortable. He had expected to confront Middleton and perhaps have a jumbled, frightened or denying reaction. Instead he had someone who knew and realised and who had not lost one iota of his self-confidence or self-esteem. Pringle knew that Gilbert Winter felt then that he had lost some of his. It was a dirty job made all the harder.

"And the other part of your task, if I mistake it not, was either to warn me off, or, if I reacted in the way you hoped, to use this information about me? Pretty low behaviour for a once great nation." Middleton looked angry. He was in full charge of the interview now.

Winter sat and said nothing. Pringle's own sympathies were disloyally creeping round to side with Middleton.

"Either I would pack up in panic and drop out of the

race or, if I were made of sterner or baser stuff, you perhaps thought I could be blackmailed, or shall we say persuaded—it's a more acceptable word, into helping you out of the present difficulties? I imagine this was your plan. Otherwise you would not have let it get this far and would have refused me Agrément from the outset, without explanation, ruining me, but hardly serving your ends in the process. Well, well. Perfidious Albion, with a very small p." Middleton was now in full swing. He turned to face Pringle. "I hope you've got all this down verbatim, young man. Your political masters should read all about it." Pringle kept his eyes on his pad and scribbled furiously. It was all going wrong, but worse was to come. He chanced a quick glance at Gilbert Winter who had regained a little of his composure but looked grey and unhappy. He was staring at Middleton.

"Well, you know Mr Winter, it's not going to work out in either of these ways. Your bet was that I would curl up and co-operate under the threat of your leaking a story to the Press on the lines of 'Once the Führer's Aide, now Mainfare's'. That right? You'd hope to get my co-operation or have the whole pack, the Washington Jewish lobby, the lot, howling for my blood, and what a setback that would be. But too bad, Mr Winter. Just too bad. You see my political sponsors know. They know all about me, and they are well briefed. At the most you may get rid of me. But to my political masters the fact that as a young officer I served my country and its ruler loyally, that I did not desert or betray, is perhaps not such an offence as you seem to consider it. Do you know what age I was when I left Berlin, Mr Winter? I was in my mid-twenties. Hardly the most responsible age. Few, very few would have that stone round my neck to pull me under, surely not even here, Mr Winter. Some sections of the press might call for my removal. But some might say otherwise. I have had a responsible and respected career in the last thirty years,

Mr Winter. Back in Washington, they agree. I offered to stand down, but they said why the hell? They'll stand by me. Do you know Mr Winter, if you use this, if you prevent my Agrément, all you'll do is plunge our bilateral relations into an even deeper abyss than they are at present. And what good will that do you, Mr Winter? You ask your political masters that."

Middleton stood up. Then he did the unexpected. He smiled.

"Goodbye, Mr Winter. Perhaps your colleague would be good enough to show me out. D'you know, Mr Winter. I'm sorry for you. You're probably ashamed right now, deep inside you. But you'll rationalise. You'll say to yourself that it wasn't you trying to destroy a man. It was a political decision, taken by your Ministers. You were only doing what you were told, in the sake of a cause you believed to be just. Now where might I have heard that argument before? Could it have been at Nuremberg."

Middleton opened the door for himself and walked out. Pringle hesitated, and then followed lamely after him.

CHAPTER SIXTEEN

Foreign and Commonwealth Office, London, S.W.1

PRINGLE SPENT THE night in bed with Helen, and the next morning taking the record while the Secretary of State discussed the whole American affair with her father. It had been a busy twenty-four hours. The Secretary of State was annoyed, the Prime Minister was very angry and was looking around for someone to blame for the embarrassment. Our Ambassador in Washington had been summoned by the American Secretary of State and spoken to in no uncertain terms at the scruffy and unworthy attempt, to quote his words, to subvert a most senior American diplomat, and an ex-Senator in addition. The Americans had, however, kept the whole thing quiet. They might feign anger, but they would also get their fair share of embarrassment if the thing got out. A man from the Führerbunker doesn't turn up as candidate for Ambassador in London every day. For good measure, the Americans called in the German Ambassador in Washington as well, and tore him off a strip too. The Americans were assuming that the Foreign Office must have had some support and information from the Federal Government. They had not until then, but the way the Americans handled the issue did the trick.

The German Ambassador came to the Office at his usual time of eleven o'clock. Pringle was sent down to meet him. He arrived in his chauffeur-driven Mercedes, and Pringle went forward to open the door for him. He climbed out. Then Pringle saw that Helen had been in the back with him. He was managing to keep his business and private lives nicely separate, and this juxtaposition of them seriously unsettled him. She saw his startled look and gave a giggle. Just-you-wait-my-girl thoughts crossed Pringle's mind.

"What's the matter, Helen," her father turned to look at her in astonishment. Then he focussed on Pringle, recognised him as the man who had helped make a fool of him, and promptly looked back at his daughter. "Is this the man you were talking about?" he asked her in German. She nodded. If Pringle had been startled, now he was embarrassed. "I see," he said. "But I'll be late for the Minister. See you at lunch." He slammed the door of the car, she gave a cheery wave to both, and the chauffeur drove her quickly away from the Office towards Horse Guard's Parade and the Mall.

"This way, Ambassador," Pringle said, opening the door for him. He did not reply, but Pringle did not expect him to.

The German Ambassador was less effusive in his greeting of the Secretary of State than last time. The Secretary of State, in his turn, was in a subdued mood. They got down to business promptly. Gilbert Winter sat quietly at one side, the Principal Private Secretary sat efficiently to the left of his Minister. The only person missing, who had been in on the last occasion, was von Sattendorf. Pringle wondered what had happened to him. The Ambassador was the type who liked to have an assistant around.

"We have been successful," began the Ambassador, "and my Foreign Minister agreed yesterday with the Chancellor himself, that the following information be passed to you in the strictest confidence." Pringle watched the man speak. He was precise and dry, so unlike Helen.

"I have a report here which unfortunately is in German. Perhaps I can try to read and translate it as I go along. But it will be a bit rough." He looked around. "I am sorry. Von Sattendorf was meant to have prepared it, but

in the circumstances..." He left the sentence incomplete.
   Pringle volunteered to save the Ambassador the trouble. He looked irritably at him, then agreed. Perhaps he thought Pringle would make a fool of himself, but translation was one of his stronger points and he may just have risen in his estimation by the end. It was in the form of what is known as a *Bout de Papier*, a diplomatic communication or report that has no official standing. It is never typed on official paper, and can therefore be disowned. Pringle read:
   "From the nature of the question put to the Ambassador by the British Secretary of State, it must already be known or suspected by Her Majesty's Government that Wilhelm Schenker the junior aide to Hitler, and the man nominated to be Ambassador of the United States to London are one and the same person. This the Federal Authorities can confirm; detailed documentary evidence is available if required. Pre-supposing, however, that this is already known to Her Majesty's Government, it will be of considerable additional interest that, on an unrelated matter, certain links exist between Schenker, a certain Professor von Neumann, resident in the Federal Republic, and a British Member of Parliament Sir Geoffrey Benner. Enquiries by the Federal Taxation Authorities, which were being conducted totally separately from this, into illegal international financial and stock-market transactions involving large-scale tax avoidance, disclosed close financial links between these three persons. Investigations, in particular the information gathered by an agent of the Tax Authorities during a recent sailing trip in the Baltic undertaken by the Professor and the British Member of Parliament, uncovered major international property deals, one of which, mentioned in the context of a sale of an estate in the American State of Pennsylvania, personally involved Schenker, or, as he is now known, Middleton. The suspected tax frauds, while important to the appro-

priate Federal Authorities, are of little relevance to this particular investigation. But the transfer of ownership of the Pennsylvanian estate certainly is. We have in our possession papers, dealing with an event which took place in August of 1967, which have considerable relevance to the background and rôle of Mr Henry Middleton. Apart from the present difficult state of American-European relations, they have a significance of fundamental importance to the Federal German Government, which Government is conscious always of its international position and reputation in relation to the tragic and inhuman events which took place during the period of the Third Reich. Attached as an annex to this note is the summary of evidence dealing with this particular Pennsylvanian estate and the ownership of it from some time in the early nineteen fifties, until late in 1967."

Pringle stopped translating, and the German Ambassador grudgingly thanked him. "You can have the annex translated and read at your leisure, Secretary of State. It makes a fascinating and important story if it is true. We had doubts about it until very recently. Now we have fewer doubts, but your assistance will be needed before we are finally sure."

"I don't quite understand, Werner," said the Secretary of State.

"I'm afraid that the latest evidence came from very close to home, Minister," said the Ambassador. "You will understand that this has just happened. It is extremely delicate and embarrassing, and final investigations have not yet been carried out."

"The Foreign Office is nothing if not discreet," said the Secretary of State.

Walter von Sattendorf was foolish and did not say 'no' to a second time. But this occasion was in London. He had gone to his new post in advance, and was living in a hotel in Chelsea. His wife and son were still at the family Schloss; he was spending more of his day looking for a suitable house for the family than he was spending at the Embassy. But he was in his office at the beginning of his second week. It was a Monday morning. The telephone rang and a voice said: "This is Heidi."

"Oh hello," he responded, slightly embarrassed. But he was not too worried. He was a temporary bachelor in a big city; there were another two weeks until his wife arrived; Heidi said she was in London for only a few days; he was lonely, and though he had been invited to several cocktails and dinners already he was finding the lack of female company a slight strain, despite the possibilities for purchased sex which were blatantly available in the British capital. He was, with all his failings, not much in favour of the commercial variety.

So Heidi it was. He met her at her hotel, just off the Strand, a small but comfortable place with anonymous rooms and clientele. He took her out to dinner. She was on holiday and was not pursuing him, she said. She had a girl friend who had gone north for a wedding for two days and this had left her at a loose end. She hoped he didn't mind her ringing? No, of course he didn't mind.

They went to a little French restaurant in Soho and ate well, and because he was on his foreign allowances he did not notice the steep charges. Afterwards they took the advice of the head waiter and ended up in a very noisy discotheque where they danced a great deal more slowly than everyone else on the floor. He grew embarrassed at the familiarity that developed between them, until he realised that absolutely no-one else would notice amid the music and the darkness. He managed to restrain himself on the floor; they left, he called a taxi, and took her back to her hotel. How informal it was after the restrictions of life in Germany.

At the hotel, fortified by the wine of the evening, he

booked a double room, ready to lie. But the night porter scarcely bothered to get him to fill in the register. Her room stayed empty for the night, but she left him at dawn and returned to it to get some sleep. He paid and left in time to return to his own Chelsea hotel to tidy up for the office. As he had another night with Heidi ahead of him, he kept the room in the hotel off the Strand booked. There was nothing like planning sin in advance.

The second evening they ate at the *Gay Hussar* in Greek Street. They sat at one of the little tables against the wall in the tiny restaurant and ate Hungarian, he pointing out to Heidi in whispers, the one or two famous faces which he already recognised. They talked seriously; indeed they talked to each other for the first and the last time. He told her in a maudlin way about his career, his ambitions, his disappointments. At times she was sorry for him, at times jealous of his family and happiness. She told him about her family, her mother struggling after the War to bring her up in a tiny village just outside Munich. Her father, she had grown up believing, had been killed in Berlin by the advancing Russians.

But in 1950, she went on, a man had come into her family life, and then there had been money and good things, and a move to a new house, and toys, and the man, the man she called Uncle. Were there not secrets in every German family? The man had gone away, but the money had remained for a while. She had found her mother crying one day. She was told that the man was her father, that he had gone and had left no forwarding address. There was another woman; there had always been another woman. Her father had been important, he had been in the centre of things, would have gone far if the War had turned out differently. But that was past.

In the mid 'fifties her mother had turned ill and her father had briefly returned. There had again been money, but he had other more important things to do, and he had left once more. This time her mother was not sad, but she was dying. Heidi had tended her night and day for three weeks. Her mother told her a story about eight men who had left Berlin in a small plane in the early hours of the morning of Sunday the twenty-ninth of April 1945. There had also been a woman and a puppy.

What was her father's name? von Sattendorf asked Heidi. He remembered seeing a name printed in the cardboard frame of an old faded photograph in her flat in Mehlem. She told him.

It was not until after they arrived back at the hotel, and after their exertions there had dissipated some of the effect of the wine, that he realised what the name Wilhelm Schenker should mean to him. Then he remembered. He remembered his Ambassador telling him about the Federal Government's own investigations, and about a mistake over the names Wolfgang and Wilhelm at the time of the British Secretary of State's enquiry. His Ambassador had been most upset by his carelessness, but he had just been dealing with the papers on the German investigation and the correct name was fresh in his mind. It was understandable.

But when he did remember, von Sattendorf began playing a different, colder game. He left Heidi briefly, went down to the porter's desk and persuaded the man, for an enormous amount of money, to produce a bottle of whisky, some ice and two glasses. He returned to the room, and played the game of getting her drunk. What was she, anyway? A slut; someone who by her dress and behaviour would sleep with and probably had slept with everyone. His judgement was wrong about that as well, but she did tell him in the end that she had come to London to meet her father.

And that, said the German Ambassador precisely, is where the British Authorities may wish to help.

CHAPTER SEVENTEEN

The Hon. Henry A. Middleton, London

WAS VON SATTENDORF ashamed of what he had done, or was he more worried about his own position? They would record all the background; it would be on his personal file; he would never feel clear of it, and his wife, his child ... Of course the Ambassador had said that they were grateful, so grateful. And the girl: would Heidi feel grateful? She would know. She would be bound to know. And then? Then what had he achieved? He had seen a name printed into the cardboard frame below a yellowed photograph. The British Secretary of State had asked his Ambassador; and then, then he had heard the name again. The name and a startling story. He had talked. Brief, very brief applause. In any case they knew all about Wilhelm Schenker already. What he had told them had been very little ... or so much. But would he not have to do the same again? Where did loyalties lie?

Von Sattendorf went with the British and Federal officials in a car, and pointed out the hotel. He gave them the room number; then he went away in disgust with himself. In Old Testament terms, the sins of the father were inherited by the child, but no-one asked him to assist and play mini-Judas to a cheap lay.

Two men went up to her room. One stood by the door. The other knocked, and when she answered he went in.

"Yes, can I help you?"

"Miss Heidi Helmich?"

"Yes."

"You are the daughter of Wilhelm Schenker?" The man in the grey raincoat spoke in a soft voice, as if this was an unwelcome experience for him.

"What do you want? Who are you? I am a visitor to London. Are you the police?" the words came rushing out in alarm.

The man repeated his question and then added: "Is this a photograph of him?"

"It is my photograph. You took it. What right have you to take it? It was in my flat, in Germany."

"When did you last see Wilhelm Schenker?" The man ignored her questions.

"That is my business." She sat down on the edge of her bed, shock written across her face.

"So you do know him? You are his daughter?"

"If I am ..." she said at last. "What right have you ... ?"

"When did you last see him?" The man was uneasy.

"1952. Perhaps 1953."

"1972. You jump twenty years?"

"No."

"Are you sure? In the Café des Artistes, in Paris on the twentieth of June, 1972?"

"No."

"Have a look at these photographs."

"If you know, then leave me alone." Heidi Helmich avoided looking at the black and white prints.

"So you did see him?"

"*Leave me alone,*" she shouted the words.

"We would like you to help us, Miss Schenker."

"Are you so ignorant? My name is Helmich."

"Yes, Miss Helmich. We would like you to help."

"Get out of my room. You should have a warrant of some sort. Where is your warrant?"

"We would like you to help us Miss ... er ... Helmich."

"Your warrant?"

"Then we will come back."

"Do so. Bring with you a statement saying why I am being questioned."

"Your passport. We have seen that it is not quite in

order." The man produced a small booklet.

"You have it from the concierge ... the Reception. What right do you ... ?"

"That is why you hand your passport in at the desk, Miss Helmich." The man paused and went over towards the window and looked out. "I ask you again. Will you help us?"

"I will contact my lawyer in the morning. I will contact the German Consul..."

"Tomorrow will be too late, Miss Helmich. Your father is booked on a plane for New York. A TWA flight, at 1120 hours tomorrow."

"Get out. Get out!" she shouted.

"I'm sorry you see fit to act this way, Miss Helmich."

"If you do not leave immediately I shall contact the German Consul..."

"Very well, Miss Helmich. But we shall be in touch." The man in the grey mackintosh left her then, shutting the bedroom door carefully behind him.

At three-thirty in the afternoon, Heidi Helmich left her hotel, walked northwards along the little street and then turned left into the turmoil of the Strand. It was a short walk to Trafalgar Square and the National Gallery, but she tied on a head scarf against the wind which carried in it a scattering of rain. She wanted to look her best. From time to time she looked round to see if anyone was following her, but she was no expert and noticed nothing.

She asked at the Information counter where she could find the famous Holbein painting called the Ambassadors, and then walked slowly through the Galleries until she located it. She looked at her watch; it was now five to four.

By no means a woman who found enjoyment in classical painting, she nonetheless found this painting fascinating. She looked in the guide book she had bought and read that the two men in the painting were the French Ambassador Jean de Dinteville and his friend George de Selve, later Bishop of Lavour, the one paying the other a visit in the spring of 1533. Behind the two men who stared out from the picture with a remarkably modern mixture of intelligence and boredom written on both faces, were shelves littered with books, musical instruments, astral and terrestrial globes. But of the whole picture, perhaps the most extraordinary part which usually escaped the normal glance, was the hugely distorted skull painted into the foreground. It was so grotesquely misshapen that it was only when one went closer and looked along the surface of the painting from the right hand side that one recognised it for what it was.

It was four o'clock. She looked round the room. There were about a dozen people there, young for the most part, probably students. A coloured security guard sat on a little upright chair in one corner, arms folded, staring intently into space. She waited.

At one end, the exhibition room was being redecorated and temporary, free-standing screens were drawn across as a partition. A painter on a high wooden trestle, balanced between two ladders, was having trouble with one of the parts of the screen. He fell against it, then regained his balance, but the screen itself fell. The man shouted a warning, there was a crash, but no-one was hurt. One of the students laughed.

At that moment Heidi Helmich saw two people: she saw a man she recognised, a startled man in a grey mackintosh, briefly revealed behind the fallen screen, and she saw another man, a man she knew as Wilhelm Schenker, coming towards her through one of the doors of the gallery. He was smiling, his hand was stretched out towards her, he was about to say something.

Unless one had been very close, one would not have heard her whispered word of warning, nor seen her make a brief gesture towards the screens as she walked straight past him, through the galleries and out into the remains of the day's grey light in Trafalgar Square. He remained where he was, staring with fierce concentration at the Holbein painting. He looked calm, but there were tears in the corners of Heidi's eyes as she walked away along the crowded pavement, realising that it would be a long time, if ever, before he contacted her, before she saw her father once again.

By five o'clock Middleton was back in the room he had been temporarily given at the American Embassy. He decided to wait there. He knew, after the incident at the National Gallery, that this time it was serious, that he would be confronted again before he left. And he had made up his mind by the time he saw his visitor.

This time Gilbert Winter was instructed to see Middleton on his own. Winter had protested; he said that it was not the proper rôle for a diplomat. But in the end he went. Pringle waited in the car outside the Embassy in Grosvenor Square. He looked up at the giant eagle above the Embassy and wondered if they had managed to fix it safely. Once there had been rumours that it was about to fall: an interesting death to be killed by a bronze eagle while crossing Grosvenor Square. He looked at the building. Not too distinguished, but with one of those clever features of disguised Embassy architecture, which do not look impressive. Round the sides there is a small ramp with stones bedded in the concrete. At the top there is a simple iron railing. Then there is a gap. Behind that, the exciting glass windows of the Embassy building itself. But take a crowd, a revolutionary crowd storming the Embassy. What do they face? A wall, a moat, an incline. It is small beer, in mediæval terms, but it makes the American Embassy in Grosvenor Square, London, West One, very much more difficult to storm.

Winter waited a long half hour in the ante-room. A half

hour to cool his heels, to give him time to reflect on the apology he was doubtless there to deliver. Then he was shown into Middleton's office. Middleton slowly finished writing something at the huge desk and did not look up. Winter waited, standing, in silence. The Assistant who had shown Winter in withdrew. It was the old one-upmanship gambit: make the suppliant wait; make sure he realises he is interrupting something more pressing, more important; make him realise that he is an unwelcome intrusion.

At length Middleton stood up. "Good afternoon, Mr Winter." They shook hands formally. "Please sit down." He gestured towards an opulent easy chair. "Would you like some coffee, American coffee, or, perhaps, a drink?"

Gilbert Winter declined. He came to the point at once, speaking in a low monotone, but nonetheless forceful for that. Middleton's attitude changed rapidly from determination to alarm. Perfidious Albion had played it slowly but had got there in the end with the whole story of the Führer's escape. It hit and it hit hard.

There was a long pause when Winter had finished speaking. Then, slowly, Middleton stood up and went across to a suitcase which was standing in the corner of his room. He put the case on a chair, unlocked it and took out a thin metal box with a combination lock. He dialled a set of numbers and opened the box. He took out two large sealed envelopes, placed one on his desk and brought the other over and handed it to Winter. Then he sat down again.

"Do not open it here, Mr Winter. There is no point. It contains a tape, and you need a recorder to play it. It is my story of the Führer's escape. It is also my insurance policy."

After Winter had left, which he did almost immediately, Middleton buzzed the Assistant on the intercom and told him he did not wish to be disturbed. He then sat at his desk for about a quarter of an hour going over the situation in his mind without panic, without fear. He had prepared for too long, and he was a methodical man.

He stood up, carefully emptied his pockets of everything in them. Wallet, diary, pen, handkerchief, credit cards and keys were placed in a pile in front of him on his desk. He took a large envelope from his drawer and placed the lot inside. He stood silently for a moment, checking. He knew his suit and other clothes contained no markings, but what else? He paused, then pulled off the thin gold wedding ring from his hand and also his large fraternity ring, and put them in the envelope along with the other things. Only his spectacles he retained. That could be done later.

He sealed the envelope and put it in the metal despatch box, closed and locked it and returned it to his suitcase which he also closed. Then, picking up the other sealed envelope which he had taken out earlier with the one he had given to Gilbert Winter, he left his room and entered that of his Assistant.

"I'm going out for a walk, Steve," he said. "Bit of a headache, and I've been here several days now and have still not walked the gold-paved streets of London. No I don't want the car, and would you make my excuses; I don't think I will make the Minister's reception; tell him you think I've gone a bit mad and have gone for a walk." He laughed cheerfully, and his Assistant laughed back. Middleton had judged correctly. His Assistant had thought for a moment that he had gone a little peculiar. But why should the future United States Ambassador to London not take a walk if he wanted to?

Middleton left the Embassy at about four o'clock. There was quite a crowd of people at the entrance, and only the Security Guard saw him go. It was a bit odd, he thought, because the new man's car was not outside. But he did nothing about it except to make a note in his log book.

Middleton, clutching a brown envelope, walked round the corner from Grosvenor Square into Upper Brook Street and along to Park Lane. There he hailed a taxi which took him to Victoria Station, and there, it was believed that the American Ambassador to be, the Hon. Henry A. Middleton, or Wilhelm Schenker, or someone with another name and identity and passport and papers contained in a plain brown envelope, took a train to one of the Channel ports.

Foreign and Commonwealth Office, London, S.W.1

Helen was at a dinner of the Anglo-German Association with her father, and Pringle was spending the night on his own. He made himself bacon and eggs at the flat and settled down to pay some long outstanding bills and catch up with other correspondence. He watched the news on television and then decided on an early night.

It was about eleven o'clock when Gilbert Winter rang. He had had a call from the Resident Clerk and was on his way in to the Office. He would be there in about half an hour, and wanted Pringle to go in too. The Resident Clerk had rung the Secretary of State and warned him that they might need to consult him during the night. Winter would say no more on the telephone. They had been given a bombshell of a tape by Middleton, they had yet to work out its full significance, but had decided about eight that evening to wait until they had a full transcript the next day.

Pringle parked in the Foreign Office Quadrangle as usual, and went into the building. It was his friend the doorkeeper on duty. "Good evening, Mr Wilson," he said. "Sorry you've had to come in at this late hour. Hope it's nothing serious."

Now was a chance to put matters right. Pringle would tell him the truth. He was not Mr Wilson; someone else was going around using his name. "Look here," he began. "There's been a misunderstanding." At that moment, Gilbert Winter came in the door after him. "Oh leave it," he said to the puzzled doorkeeper. "It'll keep."

"Yes, Mr Wilson. Of course," he said. Pringle shrugged, and followed Winter into the lift.

On the way up Winter told him. "Disappeared?" Pringle asked. "How, why?"

"Walked out of the Embassy at about four this afternoon saying he was going for a walk. The Embassy Staff have been checking round the hospitals and with the police and so on. Let them. They don't know yet. But I do, or at least I think I do."

"What do you mean, Gilbert?"

"He's done a bunk. The little we have heard of that tape tells me this for sure. It wasn't an insurance policy. His early training has stood him out the years. If he were to fall, then, like his Führer before him, he was determined that everyone would fall with him. On that tape is the evidence that not only was Senator Mainfare aware of Middleton's past in the Berlin bunker, which is neither here nor there now, but that Mainfare himself was, long before his election to the Senate, a major party to the whole plot, the escape, and all the events which ended in August, 1967. Mainfare is, without any shadow of doubt, the man constantly referred to in the evidence as the 'American Leader'."

"So what do we do? Do we act on our own, or with the Germans, or do we tell the Americans officially?"

"That's for the Secretary of State to decide. He's coming across tonight, as soon as they've voted in the House.

It may be late though; Private Office expect that the energy debate may go on till one or one-thirty."

"My sleep. And I've a heavy day tomorrow." Pringle was thinking of Helen. He had to keep fit for that girl.

"So have we all," said Winter dryly. Pringle was sure he was not thinking of Mrs Gilbert Winter.

At midnight, Terry Miller, summoned in after a dinner, turned up, and they reviewed the situation. The American Embassy were still presuming that their Ambassador designate was suffering from amnesia, had been involved in a traffic accident or something similar, and for the moment they were kept thinking that way. The police had launched an enormous search operation. The press were on to the story and, desperate for hard news for the early editions, were beseiging the News Department Duty Officer in his ground-floor room. They could leave it that way for some hours, but a press line would have to be worked out by the morning.

At one-fifteen, a Private Secretary rang. The Secretary of State had left the House. The three men went down the corridor to Private Office for the meeting. The Minister arrived a few minutes after them, looking tired. He took his place at the head of the conference table. On his right were the Minister of State and the Permanent Under Secretary who had arrived separately; Gilbert Winter, Terry Miller, the Principal Private Secretary and Pringle sat opposite.

Winter put the Minister in the picture in his dry, concise way. When he had finished, the Secretary of State thought for a moment or two, then took charge. Despite the hour, and his tiredness he was in his best form.

"I think, gentlemen, that there's been enough of our involvement in the internal affairs of the United States. The American Administration should be told the worst."

"It'll be in their best interests to sit on it, keep quiet and hope we and everyone else will forget about it, and then we'll be no better off than we were," broke in the Minister of State.

"There's no question of letting them get away with that. If they want us to sit on the story, then we should give them a clear option. We'll do so if both Mainfare and the Mainfare line are abandoned. And that shall have to be made clear to them right at the outset. We will want to see concrete results; an improvement in the whole tone of American attitudes towards Western Europe."

"A dramatic aim in exchange for sitting on a piece of history, Minister," said the Permanent Under Secretary doubtfully.

"But what a piece of history. Can you imagine the press; they would go wild. And the Allies, the French, and what about the Israelis for example?"

"All right, Secretary of State. But if they refuse?" asked the Private Under Secretary.

"We let the cat out of the bag in a big way. Pull out all the stops. But not directly. The sort of thing I have in mind is to give a quiet briefing to that Democratic Senator, what's his name? The man who's Chairman of the British American Friendship Society. He's a strong anti-Mainfare man, and best of all, he's a self-publicist. He'd love it."

"Senator Waring."

"That's the man. Waring." The Secretary of State looked pleased. "Well it's getting late, gentlemen. I'll have to clear it with the Prime Minister first, and he may want to put it to Cabinet. But I think the best course of action if they don't play ball would be to slip this man Waring a copy of the tape. The Americans like tapes these days, and judgeing from the history of the past few months, the American democratic process could be safely left to do the rest. One last question: as I understand it, we have yet to identify the date when the recording was made?"

"That's right, Secretary of State," said Terry Miller.

"Well I suppose that doesn't affect the message: Mainfare's National Socialist preferences, allegiances, but most of all his positive support for the movement come through all too clearly. What an indictment against an American Senator, and one in such a prominent and influential position as he is. If the whole story got out, it would leave the Watergate scandal out of the picture altogether. They've got used to and bored by that business, but things to do with Hitler and the War are rooted even deeper in the lives of most, in America and in Europe."

"And Middleton? Can he really just have upped-sticks and left, leaving his life, his position? And why should he want to pull Mainfare down with him?" the Minister of State broke in again.

"Middleton may turn up, but I doubt it. He'll have had his plans for such an eventuality permanently by him. He's probably half way to South America by now, to a new life, or an old life. To a man like that, liberty comes before everything. He's abandoned more than one life before. And as to why he should want to drag Mainfare with him, well perhaps we'll never know. Jealousy could be a factor. Why should one succeed while the other failed? He wanted to ensure that he did as his Führer once did and left everything in ruins behind him. *Après moi*: that mentality."

By ten the next morning the Prime Minister had agreed to the proposed course of action. Winter had gone in early with the Secretary of State to brief him. Telegrams were drafted to the British Ambassador in Washington, copied to the Embassy in Bonn so that they could keep the Federal Authorities in the picture on the intended action. The Ambassador was to see the American Secretary of State immediately. He was to confront him with all the evidence, in particular as it affected Senator Mainfare. He was to make the British point of view very clear; if the present Mainfare-orientated trend towards American isolationism and the policy of antagonism towards Europe was not checked or halted, the British Government would feel compelled, in the interest of improving Anglo-American relations, to make this information generally known. There might be problems in the short term, but in the longer term, in Her Majesty's Government's view, it could only improve matters. The Ambassador was to add that this was not a decision that rested in British hands alone, and that the German Government, embarrassing though much of the evidence might be to them, had decided, in the absence of any American assurances and working on the assumption that Mainfare was motivated by strong dislike of the present Federal Government, to act in a similar manner. He should conclude by stating, the Ambassador was instructed, that his démarche was in no way a threat. It was a matter of letting the facts speak for themselves. This piece of diplomatic drafting contained a subtlety which escaped Pringle, since the whole message was a threat. But no matter; the US Administration would realise the enormous public outcry that would follow. The Secretary of State was right; the Second World War and the presumed fate of Hitler were still too recent a memory for people throughout the world.

The Prime Minister added a footnote. Prompted by the Secretary to the Cabinet, and arguing that the Americans might not take the threat seriously enough or act quickly enough, he gave instructions that some prodding should take place. That afternoon the Secretary of State had an important secret meeting with the Editor of *The Times*. The latter was given certain background information, in the strictest confidence, to ensure that he published. The next morning, all editions of the paper carried the following unsigned article:

Western intelligence sources have, over the past few months, been piecing together a story, the implications of which, if true, would considerably alter the accepted history of the Twentieth Century. Sources very close to a number of Western Governments have decided that the time has now come to make available to the general public certain information which demonstrates that there existed a carefully coordinated escape plan whereby Adolf Hitler was to be sprung from the wreckage of his Reich at the very last moment. Carefully documented and published investigations and reports in the past have unanimously pointed to the evidence that the more formalised escape plans, which certainly existed, were abandoned by the Führer as late as the twenty-third of April, 1945. This evidence may still be correct. But new information suggests that another plan for escape was never abandoned by him nor by any of the other major leaders of the Third Reich, not least because they did not, with the possible exception of Martin Bormann, know about it.

Formulated by a number of second rankers in the Berlin bunker over these last critical days, it was a plan conceived from a wide mixture of motives. And it was to be carried out whether or not the Führer wanted or agreed to it. If he would not go willingly, he would be abducted; there were few to stand in the way by that time, particularly as it would have been a popular move among many of those who remained.

Motives were mixed. Some, perhaps the majority in the plot, had had enough; they wanted to get out of Berlin at all costs. The longer the Führer stayed, the more certain it was that the advancing Russians would raze the Capital to the ground. And if the Führer refused to leave, it was difficult if not impossible for others to do so. A few had tried earlier and had been shot for desertion. Some perhaps had the motive, more loyal to their leader, of getting him out and away to fight another day; this was the only motive that was openly expressed among the conspirators.

And then one or two were out to buy their own freedom, to get the Führer out and hand him over to the Allies once they were away from Berlin. Those last few made only the distance to the Chancellery garden where, in the early morning of 25th April, they were dragged out and shot. Despite this, the Führer went. Whether he went willingly or unwillingly, history has kept to itself, though the evidence suggests that he was unwilling, perhaps drugged, perhaps very ill after a suicide attempt that failed. The carefully contrived cover-story of his suicide, along with Eva Braun, and his subsequent incarceration, lost some credibility through the death in the bitter fighting that followed, of some planted witnesses who had been schooled as to what to say. This left its own doubts, and rightly so. For this new evidence suggests that he and a small party of followers got away to Bavaria in a small plane, and from there made their way to Spain and then on to South America.

The Editor of *The Times*, cautious of such a sensational story and suspicious of the reasons why the Foreign Secretary had planted it on him, rather let the story die after that tantalising beginning. Hitler, the article ended, was presumed to have died shortly thereafter in some South American jungle. That was an end of it, and apart from certain very senior Americans, the public took it as a strange but unsubstantiated story and turned back to Watergate and other more actual scandals of the day. After all, there was no link between it and the front page story about the continued hunt for the missing United States Ambassador designate, Mr Henry Middleton. Why should there be? The police had got nowhere, but there were mysterious reports of a man answering to his description having taken the hovercraft ferry to France from one of the Channel ports.

* * *

A number of men sat down that evening in Winter's room to listen to the whole tape. There was a power cut and they had to use candles, but the tape recorder was rigged up to work from batteries. It was a strangely effective setting to hear in the flickering light, the disembodied voice of Wilhelm Schenker telling his story in a thin tired voice.

"In the mid-nineteen-seventies it is hard for rational men to believe that the last Tzar of All the Russias, Nicholas II, was so unprepared, so misinformed and so misguided by his secret police, so unprotected by the security afforded by his vast wealth and connections that he allowed himself and all his family to be surprised by events that should not have surprised him, and later to be assassinated in that room at Ekaterinburg. Could a man alone and unaided, with a mail-order gun, shoot a President dead at Dallas? Could a British and French government coldly conspire a Suez crisis? Did a divorce alone cause the abdication of a King? Did a Führer commit suicide among the ruins of his grey Berlin bunker?

"The man who died on the thirteenth of August 1967 in a certain Private Clinic on the outskirts of Philadelphia, was born at six-thirty in the evening of the twentieth of April 1889 in the Gasthof zum Pommer in the little town of Brannau. By the twentieth of April, 1945, his fifty-sixth birthday, he had already been living for some weeks in the two-storied bunker some sixty feet below the garden of his Berlin Chancellery. There were forcefully gay birthday celebrations among his staff. On that day, his mind was not made up as to whether to leave. His propaganda chief, who that day also broadcast an ironic message of thanks to the Führer from the German people, was urging him to hold out in Berlin, but this advice came from the man who some days later poisoned his five children before he and his wife committed suicide. The others there, Eva Braun, General Burgsdorf his chief military adjutant, and Martin Bormann, urged him to adopt that very day, the already carefully formulated plan of escape by air along the ever narrowing corridor between the advancing American and Russian armies to make his last stand at the National Redoubt near Berchtesgaden where various of his Commands and Ministries had already moved.

"But he sat in his room below a painting of Frederick the Great and he hesitated. That same day, the last top-level meeting of all the major leaders of the Third Reich met in the conference room of the bunker. They were all nervous; there was a great deal of squabbling and as no smoking or drinking was allowed in the bunker, there were no easy ways to relieve the tension. Göring, Himmler, Ribbentrop, Bormann, Speer and the Service Chiefs advised unanimously that he should leave. But still he hesitated. Between then and the twenty-third, many left for the south; even his personal adjutant, Shaub, and his strange doctor, Morell, left him. With him remained the Goebbels family, Stumpfegger his surgeon, his valet Heinz Linge, and his SS adjutant Gunsche. By the evening of the twenty-third he had decided to stick it out in Berlin, and he is supposed never to have wavered in this decision from them on.

"On the twenty-fourth of April, Colonel-General Ritter von Greim, who was commander of Air Fleet Six, flew in with the young woman pilot Hanna Reitsch; the reason for his strange summons was apparently only to be told that he was now the commander of the Luftwaffe in succession to Göring. It was a high, if doubtful, honour. They braved death in their small plane, flying low over the tree tops to avoid the radar screens. The Colonel-General was wounded in the process, and the Führer came personally and told him, as von Greim lay on the operating table with Stumpfegger cutting at his leg. It was a strange journey only to receive a new command that could have been passed to him by telegraph.

"The next day, the twenty-fifth, the Russians first began shelling the Chancellery. Four days later, at about one a.m. on the morning of Sunday, twenty-ninth April, 1945, von Greim and Hanna Reitsch left in their small plane, with the futile task of arresting Heinrich Himmler for high treason. About two hours later there was the marriage to Eva Braun, with Goebbels and Bormann as the witnesses.

"There are many versions of what happened thereafter. At four a.m. on the twenty-ninth of April the Führer supposedly signed his lengthy Last Will and Testament announcing that he was going to die in the name of his cause. Early on Monday, thirtieth April, Blondi his dog was destroyed, but where was her puppy Wolf, born in March, which he used to fondle in his lap during these last days? Erich Kempa, his chauffeur, was sent out to get two hundred litres of petrol; he brought it back in jerry cans. At 3.30 on Monday, April thirtieth, 1945, a party of SS men carried two bodies out to the garden, supervised by the batman, Heinz Linge. The two heads were concealed by blankets, but on one body the black trousers and the special boots were recognised as they dangled loose. Bormann told Admiral Doenitz about the joint suicide; the latter did not announce the death till a strange twenty-four hours later. Bormann and a number of others are said to have escaped on the night of the first to second of May, 1945.

"An hour after Hanna Reitsch's plane took off in the early hours of the Sunday morning, a second, well-equipped plane followed it south. Flying low, it was spotted by a US anti-aircraft detachment, but the strange wing markings made the victorious but confused soldiers hesitate too long before firing.

"Eight men, one woman and a small puppy besides the air crew. The ruthless man, leaving behind a carnage and a misery perhaps more terrible than any one single figure in history had done before him, had a desire for self-preservation that outlasted his escape from a bullet and two hundred litres of kerosene by only a single day.

"The collapse was brief, the strained recovery held for some nine months until he realised that the egg he had created was shattered beyond repair. Physical prostration caused by unaccustomed climatic conditions followed the nervous collapse which had, as its final trigger, the death of a young dog called Wolf.

"After that flight in the small plane there had been a day near Berchtesgaden, a two week stay in a well prepared castle in hospitable Spain. Then on to a great estate bay swamp for over two and a half years. The host, German and Nazi to the core, overwhelmed with pride and devotion at first, eventually was more than glad to see the sad group leave his life. He had his estate to look after. The staff might turn. One man had, and a bullet and the fish had found him. It was a strain too great even for a great cause. And mental instability in the central figure distressed, even revolted him.

"The blonde woman had left first to an ant-ridden typhoid grave in a corner of the garden by a huge tree. The central figure had been sick over the last days and had not attended her last moaning hours, nor had he gone to the little ceremony of burial. As the few left the upturned earth, the host, the magnificent cultured host muttered, "The bitch has had her last lay," and a Spanish gravedigger who understood too much German was deeply shocked.

"With one other dead and two more disloyally fled to seek salvation elsewhere on their own, five men after two and a half long years, went north.

"Morale was low, but comfort was not lacking, and this somewhat eased the strain of the constant fear of discovery."

A candle flickered and went out. Pringle stood up to light

a new one. It was about then on the tape that Wilhelm Schenker's story turned from the impersonal to the personal. He began to tell of his own rôle in the affair, how he had flown out with the party from Berlin, how he had stayed with them until they reached the security of the Madrid sanctuary. Then he had been sent back, back into the fear and ruins of the Third Reich, equipped with a new, temporary identity, that of a young communist who had been imprisoned for his opposition to the Nazi regime, who had escaped, who had been working for its overthrow. And he went back with one main purpose, to find and bring out the hidden funds to finance the greatest escape of all time.

Schenker skimmed briefly over the dangers, the frustrations of his work over the next eight or nine months, the moments of real fear when he was on two occasions nearly uncovered by the Allied authorities, once through his own carelessness, once betrayed by a fellow German who held some of these secret funds and was more than unwilling to part with them to finance the future life of his Führer. Schenker told of a party of ten loyal men who gathered secretly one night to surround a prosperous house on the outskirts of Hamburg in which lived this man who was now co-operating to a greater or lesser degree with the Allies. The next day, those Allied Authorities briefly investigated another unexplained murder in the brutal aftermath of the War when old scores were paid off with impunity.

The bulk of Wilhelm Schenker's great work was completed when the small but heavy crates of gold were secretly ferried north first to Sweden and then on by a long and dangerous route to the coffers of a Swiss bank. Nine months later Wilhelm Schenker had rejoined the party in South America to be given a hero's welcome in return for bringing the promissory notes to an amount enough to finance a small kingdom. This wealth and a silently loyal community moved them over many borders. Near Philadelphia in Pennsylvania, a large house was bought, fortified and beautified for them by an American sympathiser, Dwight Mainfare. It was from that time that Schenker's close relationship with Mainfare dated. It was from those beginnings that the political careers of both men became inextricably cemented together.

With the passage of time, tensions over discovery were dissipated. The money was invested, and did well. A little of it disappeared and then there were only three men left, for two men were found dead in a New York warehouse, and the Mafia were blamed. There were others in the sidelines of the main arena who knew the old cause, but not even they knew of the existence of the man. Three left of the core, though, besides Mainfare, there were a dozen more in the know. It was a new dedication, a new secret now. Of the three, one more died, but he was old, the death was from natural causes, and the body was flown home to the Rhineland for burial. Of those who left Berlin in the early hours of twenty-ninth April, 1945, only two men were left by March 1962. A middle-aged man and an old man, a geriatric mumbling case, almost bald, with a shaven upper lip. The right arm and hand were so withered and twisted, could they once have stretched out and up at a defiant forty-five degrees; could that hand have bent backwards in an awkward skew salute?

But the body must have had some hidden, inner resilience to outlast nearly all the others. It took five and a half more years, until August, 1967, before the Führer of the Third Reich, Adolf Hitler, born Schicklgrüber, died in that Philadelphia clinic of a complex pulmonary failure at the age of seventy-eight.

As the men sat listening in the flickering candle light, the last words that came from the tape recorder were: "And I was there when the end came."

* * *

But while the tape ended there, the younger of the two men, Wilhelm Schenker's story had continued. As far as the British authorities were concerned, he had been only a name on a card in an office in Lower Regent Street, London S.W.1. He had also been a name on cards in the Documentation Centre in Berlin, in an office in Vienna, and in a computer in Washington. He was listed as a link man in the neo-Nazi movement. But no one bothered much about digging out such cards in the late 'sixties. He had nothing to do with nuclear weapons nor strategic secrets nor the Cold War; there was no money nor interest nor effort available to investigate such smaller delinquents, though they had been party to the sins of the Third Reich.

It was three or four years later that the identity of the companion of the man who died began to interest a very small number of people within the Western Intelligence community. Around the end of 1970 there was evidence to suggest that a branch of Israeli Intelligence also had begun to show some interest. But, for reasons unknown, the American agencies which in March, 1962, and again in September, 1967, began making similar discreet investigations abandoned their efforts to do so, following a directive which reportedly came from the top. Until January, 1972, while the existence of Wilhelm Schenker was known about in these limited circles, there were many gaps in the dossier, including the fact that he had once been an assistant adjutant to the Führer or, even less so, that the Führer might have been alive, in body if not in mind, as late as the thirteenth of August, 1967.

They sat together after the tape had run its course and discussed its story more as a human document than as a political testament or in relation to how they were going to use it. A sentence on the tape around the time when Schenker was telling about Mainfare's provision of the

Pennsylvanian estate explained why he had decided to bring Mainfare down with him when he disappeared. It was a throwaway line about Mainfare never really having been a Nazi, never having had the opportunity to realise what the war was all about, sitting in the security of the United States. He had not suffered for the Cause; he was not even a German, but despite this, he had taken charge when the little party had first arrived from South America. And he had remained in charge. Schenker said nothing explicit but the man that was revealed by the tape showed that this had left its mark; there had been something akin to jealousy that an outsider should be in command. While Schenker remained close by Mainfare's side that was a supportable situation, but now what remained of the organisation could not be run by someone who did not really belong.

The British Ambassador passed over a copy of the tape the next day. If this failed to have an effect, the Secretary of State would speak to Senator Waring. He would reveal that Wilhelm Schenker and Henry Middleton were one and the same. With Middleton's continued non-appearance, the media would have a field day. Sometime after, if more pressure was needed, the Senator might agree to hold a press conference in Washington, and announce that he had tape-recorded evidence which proved that as far back as August 1967, and almost certainly well before that, the chief colleague, collaborator and patron of Henry Middleton had been Senator Dwight Mainfare, and that the title deeds of a certain Pennsylvanian estate had, at the time of Hitler's death at a clinic near there on the thirteenth of August, 1967, been in the possession of the self-same Senator.

One might speculate on the words with which Senator Waring might end his press conference, words that would send every reporter in the room rushing to the nearest telex and telephone.

"The blame, gentlemen, is not that previous Administrations failed to uncover the greatest escape of all history, the escape of the greatest single enemy this country has ever known. Not that they failed to discover that he lived among us in peace and security for many years. But there is blame that a man, a figure central to this present Administration, knew of this fact, was party to its concealment, was predominant in its successful outcome. In consequence, this man must be judged by all fair men as being totally and absolutely unfit to hold the high office that is presently his."

Those words were never spoken. There was no need for them. The United States Administration had too many problems to cope with in that month and in the months that followed. There was only routine regret when a Senator was rapidly nudged into resigning due to ill-health, and moving from there into forced obscurity. For what was one Senator Dwight Mainfare to stand in the way of what a President later and publicly called "that greatest and most important of all links extending between the people of the world today, that bond, that series of bonds, which binds the United States of America with its friends and allies throughout Western Europe."

Thus the words of diplomacy.

"Why were you christened Helen; why not Helena?"

"Mother was English, didn't I say?" She was curled up beside Pringle in her usual manner, hair streaming down her face in a way he found continuously appealing. She was wearing his towelling dressing-gown again, half fastened by the belt round her waist.

"They met just before the war, and married as soon as they got in contact again after it. Helluva fuss in Mother's family, marrying a German and so on. And she used to be in the Foreign Office too. So you see, you and I are linked professionally."

"Professional, eh?"

"D'you think I'm amateur, then? Is that all the gratitude?" She made a grab at him, and, as was the nature of their relationship, that was the end of any serious conversation for the next hour or so. Then she got up and made coffee for them both, and they sat drinking it.

"D'you think he'll turn up again?" she asked.

"Who?"

"Middleton. I met him with Daddy the other day. I thought he was rather nice. Very distinguished looking." She knew most of the story now.

"I should think not," he said, quoting Gilbert Winter. "And without him there is no final proof."

"But what makes a man like Middleton, or Schenker just give up and float away without a fight? He had so much to lose."

"In the long run he had more to gain. And he's not going off to live in a garret somewhere. The bet is he's already drinking Planter's Punch and crunching cashew nuts with his buddies in great comfort somewhere. He'll have stashed away a lot of money and it's just been sitting there waiting for him along with his new name, personality, and life. A very agreeable retirement with wine, women and the Horst Wessel song round the fire of an evening."

"What about a man like your Sir Geoffrey Benner? Why does he break after so many years? Thirty years of silence and then he spills all the beans?"

"He was presented with a *fait* almost *accompli*. He tried to be a Quisling and failed. He had no option this time, and he hasn't got a South American estate to fall back on. He has his safe constituency seat, which he'll continue to have and to hold for the few years left before he retires. I find that very understandable. He admitted only to the inevitable. And he was better off helping a little and getting away with a lot. We're not going any further with him, whether he knew the whole Hitler story or not. He got off lightly."

"There's another important thing that hasn't been developed properly," Helen went on, with a face that was just too solemn. "I find you revoltingly self-complacent, and far too attractive."

"Oh yes? Well I'm glad about the last bit. I thought you just behaved that way to get my money. I can't think what other reason..."

She leapt on Pringle then, and he had one of the answers all over again.

Epilogue

WILHELM STAINTON PULLED himself rather more upright in his chair by the marble pillar and watched the bustle of people passing along the corridor. Few of them looked at him. When they did, they saw a tall, well-kept old gentleman of perhaps about seventy, neatly dressed in an old-fashioned double-breasted suit, dark material with a sober stripe in it, a white shirt and perfectly knotted silk tie. The white handkerchief in the breast pocket overflowed a little too much, to indicate a daring flamboyance. The pointed shoes were carefully polished.

Mr Stainton felt a little tired that morning, but still alert and attentive. Perhaps it was the high mountain air. He crossed his legs carefully to avoid spoiling the crease in his trousers, and watched a pretty young blonde girl he had noticed once before tripping past in an attractively short skirt. Behind her came an Indian woman pushing a metal trolley containing cans. It looked heavy. He uncrossed his legs again. Nowadays he could not keep them crossed for long without getting pins and needles in them. He shot the cuff of his white shirt up a fraction and looked at his watch. It was quarter to twelve. The newspapers should have arrived.

He stood up slowly, testing each leg carefully before putting his full weight on it. Then he pushed his chair back very slightly so that it was partially hidden behind the pillar; he liked that particular seat. It was an excellent vantage point from which he could watch the world go by without exposing himself too much to everyone's gaze. With any luck, he would be back within ten minutes and no-one should have taken it by then.

He walked slowly along a corridor, down a few steps, holding on to the handrail as he went. There was a large hall and the newspaper kiosk was at the far side of it. One or two people were standing waiting. As he watched, they moved to stand in a sort of queue. Good, the papers had arrived.

He waited his turn. Service was slow. There was a man in front who seemed to be buying up everything. Then he did not have enough money. The kiosk woman got annoyed and the customer looked upset. Not quite right in the head, Mr Stainton said to himself. He looked impatiently round the hall as he waited; there were workmen everywhere putting up carnival decorations. Dear, dear, was it that time of year already; and it was so much noisier here than he remembered it had been in the old days, back home. Still, the girl would be pleased. She would come and see him and tell him how used she was to it all now. He often wondered that she wasn't just waiting to go back...

Pulling himself together with a start, Mr Stainton found himself at the head of the queue. He asked for the London *Times* and the *Frankfurter Allgemeine*. The woman unwrapped them from their airmail wrappings for him. He paid her and walked slowly back across the hall and then stopped for a moment just short of the foot of the stairs. He folded the German newspaper carefully and tucked it under his arm. Then, ignoring the news pages of *The Times*, he turned to the page just past the centre fold of the paper. Like many elderly people he was a traditionalist, and his favourite reading was the Court Circular.

Buckingham Palace: the tenth of February.
"His Excellency the Honorable James A. Friedman was received in audience today by Her Majesty The Queen and presented the Letters of Recall of his predecessor and his

own Letters of Credence as Ambassador Extraordinary and Plenipotentiary from the United States of America to the Court of St James."

How very nice for Mr James A. Friedman, thought Mr Stainton. It must give a man a real kick to be appointed to a post like that. He cast his eye across the page to his other favourite reading material, the obituaries. He very nearly did not recognise the name Geoffrey Benner, the former Member of Parliament who had retired several years ago. That was the thing about obituaries; they were always so kind, so selective in what they said.

"Oh dear, oh dear," said Mr Stainton out loud. A young gentleman who was passing stopped and asked him if he was all right.

"Oh ... oh, yes ... yes thank you very much indeed," said Mr Stainton very quickly. "Just a bit of bad news that's all."

"I'm so sorry," said the young gentleman. He looked concerned. A nice looking man and very polite. So unusual these days. He folded *The Times* up thoughtfully. Oh dear, oh dear, he said again, but this time to himself.

Mr Stainton went on his way. Up the steps and along the corridor to his seat by the pillar. The view of the mountains was glorious from there.

But the seat was pulled forward again. In the chair was sitting a middle-aged woman with dyed blonde hair. She was knitting something with fuzzy pink wool. She had a sort of smirk on her face as if she realised that she had taken his chair, as if she knew it would annoy him. But she could not possibly know.

For a second time Mr Stainton was upset, but not too upset. He was also quite determined. There was a time and a place for everything. He turned and walked purposefully back along the corridor and stopped at a polished wooden door. There was a name-plate on the door and a typewritten notice which said please knock and wait. Mr

Stainton disregarded this, gave the briefest of taps and walked straight in.

The man at the desk looked up as he entered.

"Why good morning, Mr Stainton. What an unexpected pleasure. How are you? What a fine morning it is to be sure. What a pity we can't be outside enjoying it."

"Quite," said Mr Stainton brusquely, sitting down unasked on a leather chair opposite the man's desk. "But I haven't come to pass the time of day, Möller. You know that I have better things to do, as I'm sure you have."

"Yes indeed," said Möller. "But if I can help in any way..."

"That's why I'm here." Mr Stainton thought he could detect a note of nervousness, or apprehension in Möller's manner. Well, he had a lot to answer for.

"The plane," said Mr Stainton.

"Ah yes, the plane."

"Revoltingly cramped, and the pilot must have been drunk or something. A very bumpy journey indeed."

"Yes of course, Mr Stainton."

"I must say that the discourtesy I was subsequently shown was most unpleasant, and I have come here this morning to ask you to do something about it. I am sure if *he* knew, he would not tolerate this situation for one instant. After all, it was my doing in the first place. I made all the arrangements. Most ungrateful, don't you think?"

"Most, Mr Stainton. I quite agree. We'll have to see what we can do. Now if you wouldn't mind waiting next door in my secretary's room, I'll see if I can rectify matters at once. Please..." Möller opened a glass connecting door to his secretary's office. The other room was empty. "Would you mind waiting here just a moment or two, Mr Stainton?"

"Very well, but please be quick, Möller. I've had enough of this," Mr Stainton said severely.

"Of course, Mr Stainton."

The man called Möller carefully shut the glass door, waited for a moment to make sure that Mr Stainton had settled down in the next room and was not listening outside; then he picked up a phone on the desk.

"Operator, get me Station Three." There was a pause. "Hullo? Is that Station Three? Sister Fernandez. Is that you? Look here Sister, this isn't good enough. I have old man Stainton here moaning at me on the usual net. Did you forget to give him his injection this morning? Look at the register at once. Yes, I'll wait. You really must be more careful, Sister."